KU-001-747

LV 21559937

Liverpool Libraries

GUNS IN OREGON

GUNS IN OREGON

A Western Duo

LAURAN PAINE

SAGEBRUSH
Large Print Westerns

Copyright © Mona Paine, 2004

First published in Great Britain by ISIS Publishing Ltd.,
First published in the United States by Five Star Westerns

Published in Large Print 2006 by ISIS Publishing Ltd.,
7 Centremead, Osney Mead, Oxford OX2 0ES
United Kingdom
by arrangement with
Golden West Literary Agency

All rights reserved

The moral right of the author has been asserted

British Library Cataloguing in Publication Data
Paine, Lauran
  Guns in Oregon: a western duo. –
  Large print ed. –
  (Sagebrush Western series)
  1. Western stories
  2. Large type books
  I. Title
  II. Paine, Lauran. For vengeance alone
  813.5'4 [F]

ULV 6.11.06

ISBN 0–7531–7552–5 (hb)

Printed and bound in Great Britain by
T. J. International Ltd., Padstow, Cornwall

Additional copyright information:

"For Vengeance Alone" first appeared in *Famous Western*
(6/56). Copyright © 1956 by Columbia Publications, Inc.
Copyright © renewed 1984 by Lauran Paine.
Copyright © 2004 by Mona Paine for restored material.

Table of Contents

For Vengeance Alone.....................................1

Guns in Oregon..49

FOR
VENGEANCE
ALONE

CHAPTER
ONE

Lodgepole was a small hub of buildings, garnished by an immense sea of land that rolled and ebbed off toward the horizon; there, shadowy, jagged mountains rose up out of the land and acted as a buffer and a chain of sentries between the town's homeliness and the world beyond. As a town, or village, Lodgepole left much to be desired, but, even so, it had that evasive, errant something that draws men — and women, too — to towns. Maybe it was the need for groceries, beans and flour and coffee, but if that was so, then why did they stay in town after they were through shopping? No, Lodgepole, like other little frontier settlements, was more than a town. It was a state of mind — a compelling urge within its scattered citizens — tossed by their own peculiar fates out across the ageless rangeland — to congregate and visit and talk.

Parson Rigby sat in the shade of his honeysuckle arbor, and his eyes were grave and pensive. He felt not alone exactly, but certainly lonely in the tremendous sweep of the earth that waved its first springtime shoots of wiry, tough buffalo grass at him from as far, and much farther, than he could see. The parson was a raw-boned, youngish man with gentle, wistful eyes. He didn't condemn his mission for sending him to Lodgepole; he was too good a Christian for that. But he did wish they'd sent him somewhere else where souls were easier to save, and not quite so barbaric.

He leaned back against the stiff, unrelenting green hide that was the back of his chair. There was a saying about "a little bit of knowledge being more dangerous than a lot". It was true in another sense, too, a little bit of civilization was more dangerous than a lot of civilization. In Lodgepole — where the men swore mightily, carried guns swinging rhythmically at their hips, stomped thresholds with scuffed, callused feet enclosed in boots that jingled musically with heavy, cruel spurs adorned with inlaid silver — there was little room for anything except harshness.

The parson was new to the West and its jarring intimacy and idiosyncrasies had fairly taken his breath away. He was like a little boy who was suddenly pushed into the dark — awed, uneasy, and not a little frightened, but, too, there was something away down inside of him that couldn't be completely stifled. He felt a rising well of kinship with the glories of the land and the strict, unbending code of the West.

The parson was lost in his somber reveries when he noticed a man riding into Lodgepole from the south. Every stranger was an interesting study to Rigby and he looked this one over with the professional interest of a confirmed soul-saver. The rider looked like the others. From the dented crown of his adobe-colored Stetson — gray with dust and alkali powder — to his ornate California spurs, he was a Westerner. His face was broad, clean-looking, and wary. Rigby nodded to himself. Naturally the stranger would have to be like

4

the others; no one but a plainsman would deliberately ride to Lodgepole. This man, like the others, did things without thinking ahead. They weren't necessarily mean or cruel, any of them, but just foolish — with the harebrained lack of tact that set them apart as a species.

He shrugged to himself. Very often the difference between being deliberately bad, and just plain foolish, was slight; maybe there wasn't a difference between the two of them at all, because the results were nearly always the same. The parson was surprised, though, when the rider tied up at his fence, loosened his front cinch as if he meant to stay a while, kicked open the sagging, warped gate, and entered the scraggly yard before the house.

Very deliberately the man swung up the little plank walk toward where Rigby was sitting. The parson got up and waited; he was curious. None of the cowmen or the riders came to see him alone. They didn't exactly avoid him, but, unless their wives were with them, they just didn't come visiting very often. And even with their wives along, they never acted at ease or comfortable.

"Parson Rigby?"

The man's voice was soft, well-modulated. Rigby sensed something in this man that was different, after all. He nodded with a smile and motioned toward a bench beside him. The stranger thumbed his sweat-stained hat to the back of his head and some auburn hair showed, damp and clinging, on his forehead where the skin was whiter than the face below it. The man sank down to the bench, reached deliberately into a shirt pocket, fished out a tobacco

5

sack, and held it hesitatingly for a moment as his deep-set, thoughtful gray eyes looked up.

"Mind?"

"Not at all." Rigby knew the ways of these people. When the stranger was good and ready, he'd introduce himself and get down to business. It apparently was a custom they'd adopted from the Indians — never hurry, never lose your dignity. He watched the man roll his cigarette, light it, and exhale a fragrant cloud of bluish smoke into the clear, warm air.

"My name's Webb, Mark Webb."

Webb apparently was going to say more, but Rigby interrupted him with an outstretched hand and a smile. "I'm glad to know you, Mister Webb." Webb looked a little startled and embarrassed, but he dutifully pumped the parson's white hand and dropped it.

"I was just passing through this country, on my way to Nogales, when I was stopped by a girl a few miles south of here, an' asked if I'd ride to Lodgepole an' ask you to come right quick to the Rafter L spread."

Rigby knew what the message meant. Old Bob Lambert had been dying for several months, the result of a rifle ball in his back. Apparently he was very near the end now. Sally Lambert had met the stranger, asked him to come to the parson with the message, and quite likely had gone back to the Rafter L to wait. He brought his eyes back to the cowboy and nodded slowly. "Bob's near the end of the trail."

He said it matter-of-factly, sadly, and the cowboy nodded, too. "Yeah. I figured it was something like that."

6

"Do you know the Lamberts?"

Webb flushed a little. "No," he said ruefully, "but folks don't usually send for the sky pilot unless it's a birth or a death. The girl wasn't wearin' no weddin' ring, so I figured someone in her family was cashin' in."

Rigby nodded approvingly. Mark Webb fitted into the mold the parson had mentally built for him — observant, quiet, and very deadly. But he couldn't shake off the feeling that Webb was different some way, too. He mused aloud as the sun baked into his shoulders and the honeysuckle spread its ambrosia through the dry air.

"Bob Lambert's been a big man in this country. He's one of the old-timers, Indian fighter and all that. Pretty wealthy too, I'm told. His wife died several years ago, and Sally's been all that's left to him outside of his cattle and his thousands of acres."

Webb was listening with casual interest. "What's he dyin' from?"

"Some months back, he went out to look over his stock . . . to see how far they were drifting, I guess. When he came back, he was draped over his horse, half conscious. Someone had shot him from ambush and the ball nicked his backbone and went on into his insides. He didn't know who did it, and no one else has been able to figure it out . . . including Sheriff Molden."

"No stock run off? No bad blood? No robbery?" Webb's eyes were puckered at the edges.

Rigby sighed as he got up. "No reason at all, so far as anyone can figure out." He started to move toward his little barn behind the house, hesitated, and faced Webb. "But the bullet's in too risky a spot to be removed and Bob's been slowly dying from it. I guess his time has come now."

Mark Webb got up, flicked the cigarette away, and looked down at his sinewy hands. "Well, dammit, I wish I knew what to say, Parson, but I don't, so I'll just drift." They shook hands, and the rider went back to his horse, tightened his cinch, swung aboard, and turned casually toward the main section of Lodgepole. It was too late to head back out across country anyway; the afternoon sun was sliding toward the distant peaks, so he rode to the Gregg House, tied up, went in, and registered. Then he took his horse to a livery barn before he went to his room and flopped on the hard, bumpy bed, eyes wide open and staring at the fly-specked ceiling.

After five months, going after wild horses over on the Llano Estacado, the girl was like a breath of fresh air. He pushed his arms under his head and stared harder at the ceiling. Even Nogales wouldn't have anything like her. He thought of the parson and grinned wryly. It'd been a long time since he'd seen one, a lot longer since he'd talked to one. His thoughts swung to the dying man. Why in hell would someone just shoot a man in the back? People just didn't go around shooting other people without a reason; it's too risky a pastime. The old fellow must have made a damned good enemy.

Lord, but that girl was beautiful. Her hair was like fresh taffy and she rode a horse like it was part of her. He'd never forget how she came loping up out of the dead distance of the endless range. He'd been startled for a moment at seeing anyone, but when she got closer and stopped and talked to him, his eyes had drunk in the sight of her like a man dying of thirst. He grunted, shoved himself off the disagreeable bed, and started to strip. That's all civilization was good for, anyway — beds and warm baths.

CHAPTER
TWO

The night was pleasant and fragrant when he went out on the Gregg House's porch and slumped into a vacant rocker after a mediocre dinner of liver and onions. Lights flickered and beckoned with orange fingers from the saloons and dance halls and blinked out, one at a time, from the commercial establishments. It was nice to sit in the warm gloom like a shadow and watch the trickle of humanity that flowed across the dusty roadway and on the cracked, weathered plank sidewalk. Mark Webb rolled a cigarette and let the sense of well-being that having a bath always brought to him completely encompass him with its feeling of stolen luxury.

There were other chairs on the verandah, and other men sat in them, dark silhouettes in the late dusk. Webb could smell their pipes, cigars, and cigarettes. They seemed relaxed, too, and in their drowsiness he felt companionship — although he had spoken to no one since registering. Civilization didn't seem such a bad thing from the comfort and gloomy security of the verandah, but his thoughtful eyes looked at the saloon lights and a cynical hardness flitted across them. In those smelly, noisy rooms were human wolves waiting for the kill. That, too, was a part of civilization.

10

Several of the other rocker occupants had drifted inside and that made Mark think that perhaps it was getting late. He settled deeper into his chair and the urgent, compelling face of Sally Lambert came up out of his memory again. He inspected it objectively, there in the darkness, with complete safety, and the closer he looked, the less fault he could find. There was no denying it; she was the most beautiful woman he had ever seen.

Mark was so completely lost in his reverie that he didn't notice the man walking up the verandah steps. He didn't notice him at all until a hand was laid on his shoulder, then he started half out of his chair and his holstered .45 was cool and reassuring under his fingers.

"Mister Webb?"

Mark sank back slowly, irritably. The parson. Bad enough to have his daydream interrupted, but to be startled half out of his wits was worse. He was on the verge of spitting out an unpleasant comment about the foolishness of creeping up on people, when the parson sat down and leaned forward as he spoke. "It was a shot in the dark."

Mark nodded to himself grimly; it damned near was that, all right.

"But I thought I might find you here, so I rode over," continued Rigby.

"Well, your guess was pretty good at that, Parson. After I left you, I figured it was too late to head back, so I came on in an' got a bath an' a dinner." He

11

thought of the parson's visit to the dying man. "How's your patient?"

Rigby's elbows rested on his upper legs as he leaned forward. "Not quite as bad as Sally thought he was, but he's no better. Ah, Mister Webb . . ."

That "Mister Webb" business was beginning to rankle a little. "Parson, just call me Mark, will you? Every time you say Mister Webb, I want to look around an' see if my dad's standin' behind me."

Rigby smiled weakly at the intended humor. "All right, Mark." He let a two-second lapse intervene. "I have a question to ask you."

"Yeah? Fire away."

"Would you find it convenient, since you apparently aren't working right now, to hire out to the Rafter L?"

She had liked what she saw, too; it must be that, because he hadn't met her father. In fact, he hadn't met anyone else all day long as he rode over the range. "Does she . . . I mean does Miss Lambert need a rider?"

"She needs more than that, Mark. She needs help and guidance and comfort. I can give her spiritual guidance and comfort, but I know less than nothing about cattle, and I'd rather hoped you'd help me in that."

"Then the idea was yours, not hers?"

"Yes, but she agreed that she'd have to find someone to work on the ranch steady, now that her father can't."

Another cigarette was in the making, and the hands that rolled it were oddly damp with perspiration. There was a shot of irritation and self-reproach running lightly through the cowboy. He'd been silly to presume. To hell with it; he was going to Nogales where he had friends. He wasn't going to bury himself in an adobe and mud-wattle pigsty like Lodgepole — not even for the most beautiful, most desirable, most wonderful woman he'd ever seen in his life.

"I'll ride out there first thing in the mornin', Parson, an' talk to the girl."

Rigby left with a light step and a small smile. The ways of the Lord were good. The Rafter L would have a man at the helm again, and, unless he was very much mistaken, it would have just the kind of a man it needed. Fearless, capable, and dogged. The parson meant to arise early and ride out with Mark and introduce him to Sally. He felt particularly good — so good, in fact, that when he got to his cottage and made a pot of coffee prior to going to bed, he poured a dab of rum in it before he drank it. The parson felt kindness toward Lodgepole and its rough citizens as he got into bed, and for the first time since coming West he was conscious of really contributing something tangible to the woes of his domain.

When Rigby's fat mare stopped before the Rafter L's rambling old adobe house, the parson felt a twinge of disappointment. Tied in the shade of a tired-looking old olive tree was the leggy and lean gelding bearing the plain, sloping-cantled saddle of Mark Webb. He recognized them even before Sally Lambert and Webb came off the verandah to welcome him. His disappointment passed quickly when he saw the

13

radiant look on the girl's face and the wary smile the cowboy wore.

"Parson, you're wonderful. I had no idea you were so forceful. Why, I was hardly up before Mister Webb rode in."

Rigby caught the "Mister" and looked at the pained cowboy with high amusement. He spoke as he swung off the gray mare, which was already closing her placid eyes, preparatory to a little nap in the warm morning sunlight. "Sally, he distinctly doesn't like being called Mister. May I suggest you call him just plain Mark?"

Mark was standing a little to one side of, and behind, the girl. He saw the flecks of gold sparkle in her taffy hair as she swung her head around good-naturedly and a little wave of admiration got out of control and swished around inside of him. "Is that true, Mister Webb . . . er, Mark?"

He nodded, smiling, and the three of them entered the cool old house.

The parson looked inquiringly at the girl. "Has he met Bob yet?"

"No, Dad's still not awake. In fact, I'm ashamed to say it, but I haven't been up long enough to get any breakfast." She faced Mark, and he noticed that her eyes were not more than three inches lower than his. "Mister . . . ah . . . Mark, won't you and the parson have some breakfast with me?"

She didn't wait for the self-conscious nods of the two men before she was walking toward the kitchen. "Make yourselves comfortable, gentlemen. I'll have it ready in a jiffy."

Mark looked at the minister, and Rigby looked at the cowboy. Mark shrugged and sank into an old leather chair while the parson sat on the edge of an occasional chair made of age-darkened hickory. Somewhere in the back of the house a bell rang softly and Sally Lambert swished through the room with a smile. The parson watched her go by and turned to Mark. "That's Bob's hand bell. He's awake."

Mark nodded and thought to himself that it would be quite a feat for a man to ring a bell if he wasn't awake. Sally came to the doorway and beckoned. "Dad wants to see you two."

They followed the girl to the sick room, where a large, raw-boned old man was lying perfectly flat in an old, black mahogany bed, with only the outlines of the covers to show that, once, there had been a massive and powerful body behind the drive and impulses of Bob Lambert. His blue eyes were large and direct and Mark recognized Sally's features there in the weathered, seamed old face beneath the shock of disheveled white hair.

"This is Mark Webb, Dad. You know Parson Rigby." The eyes were clear and questioning, which was a surprise to Mark, who had expected a half-conscious, quivering man in the throes of a lingering death.

"Glad to know you, Mark. Sit down, gentlemen."

They sat in silence, and Sally left the room. The man's eyes made a rapid appraisal of Mark, and swung to Rigby. "Well, Parson, it was right considerate of you to get this man for us. Lord knows we need a good man."

The frosty blue eyes ran quickly over Mark's frame again. "Well, young man, you look like you'll do." Mark blushed uncomfortably under the direct stare.

"It's not hard work. Not until we round up, then we'll get extra hands. But it does take a lot of ridin' to keep Rafter L cattle from driftin' too far away." The shrewd eyes were a little grim as he continued. "Then, of course, there's the chance of gettin' a slug in the back, an' that's generally enough to make an *hombre* keep his eyes open, ain't it?"

Mark wanted to laugh at the old man's laconic statement and dry humor. He found himself warming up to Bob Lambert. "Well, it'll keep me from stayin' too long in one place when I'm ridin', anyway."

Lambert's pale face grinned a tiny bit. He, too, liked grim humor and he liked something else, when he saw it, and now it was sitting on a chair next to his bed. Courage.

CHAPTER
THREE

Sally called them to breakfast and they left the wounded man. Mark felt a distinct twinge of pity as he walked into the kitchen where both he and the parson washed, slicked down their hair, and plunked into hard-seated chairs at the kitchen table. Sally poured the coffee, and the men ate. Mark couldn't shake off the feeling of anger that possessed him; bushwhacking was the lowest, sneakiest form of shooting he could think of. Finally he put the knife and fork down and looked at Sally. "Who the devil would do a thing like that?" He jerked his head in the direction of her father's room.

She shrugged curtly. "I'd like to know."

Mark was frowning. "Sally, people don't just go ridin' around blastin' other folk for sport. There's a reason somewhere, an' you or your dad ought to have an idea about it."

Sally Lambert understood the frustration and irritation in Mark's voice and her own heavy eyebrows drew into a slight frown. "Well, we don't. Dad was riding toward the border, looking for cattle that might get too close to the Mexican line. If strays drift over into Mexico, it takes a lot of red tape to get 'em back, so we always try to see that they don't get that far south. He didn't find any Rafter L cattle, and was coming home by way of Tiburcio Rocks when someone shot him. He managed to hang on until he got home and that's all we know about it."

Mark was building his inevitable cigarette. "Where's Tiburcio Rocks?"

"About two miles southwest. It's a jumble of rocks that makes a small hill. That's undoubtedly where the assassin hid. It's about the only place on our range where a man could hide himself and a horse. The rest of our land is open."

"Does your land run to the border?"

"Yes; as soon as we've finished eating, I'll ride the ranch with you, an' then you'll know what's Rafter L and what isn't."

Parson Rigby sat on his gray mare with a comfortably bulging paunch. Being a bachelor, he had made excellent use of his time at the Rafter L breakfast table. A truly benevolent smile was on his face as he waved goodbye to Sally Lambert and Mark, and he headed back for Lodgepole while they swung away for their ride of the Rafter L domain.

Mark approved of the cattle he saw. They were in good flesh and fetlock deep in rich grass. The bulls were breedy, the cows picked commercial-grade critters, and the calves, clean and frisky, showed the playful, curious disposition that proves their parents are getting plenty to eat. He nodded to himself. Bob Lambert may have been an old-timer in the Lodgepole country, but he certainly wasn't hidebound like most old-timers. His ranch and his livestock showed that he was a modern cowman.

Mark was so absorbed with the cattle and the great expanse of Rafter L grass that, when Sally spoke, he started slightly in the saddle. "There's Tiburcio Rocks."

Mark rode among the boulders, apparently dumped there by a whimsical, prehistoric destiny — for nowhere else, as far as the eye could see, were there any boulders on the prairie. He dismounted and poked with his boot toe among the shale. He suddenly caught sight of the glitter that he'd been looking for, bent over, and retrieved a brass cartridge.

Sally came up closely beside him and stared, wide-eyed, at the sinister little object lying in the palm of Mark's hand. He flicked it over and grunted.

"What is it?"

Mark's narrowed eyes studied the cartridge case a second longer before he stowed it in a shirt pocket and turned toward the girl. "It tells us one thing, anyway. The bushwhacker was a Mexican."

"How do you know?"

"*Gringos* don't use Mauser rifles."

They rode in silence for a long time. The range they were riding was free of cattle, and Sally pointed to little, sun-blistered, white posts stuck up at intervals across the range.

"Those are the United States-Mexican border markers. On the other side is Mexico."

Mark looked indifferently at the markers. "Did your pa ever bump into any Mex *alambristas* . . . smugglers or rustlers?"

"Oh, yes. Dad's been in this country most of his life, and in that time he's seen 'em come and go. But we don't think it was a spite shooting. The renegades Dad's tangled with are all old men now . . . as old as he is . . . and he hasn't seen any outlaws at all for ten years or so."

"This part of the border's pretty quiet, then, huh?"

"Yes, Sheriff Molden at Lodgepole, the United States Marshal at Nogales, and the Mexican *Rurales* all patrol it. Even so, though, they don't have much to do any more. There haven't been any smugglers or revolutionists cross here for years."

Mark's eyes were grave and thoughtful. "Let's get back to the ranch, shall we?"

Mark left the girl at the house, where he wrote a long and laboriously articulate letter — for him — and asked Sally to take it to Lodgepole and mail it. He explained that it was to friends in Nogales, telling them that he'd been detained *en route*.

It took several days to familiarize himself with the Rafter L, and the more he saw of the great, sprawling ranch, the better Mark liked it. In the evenings, when Sally had the hissing, brilliant lanterns going, Webb spent his time alternately playing cards with Sally and standing at the end of Bob Lambert's bed — first on one foot, then the other — talking and listening to the wounded man. Lambert couldn't raise his head, and Mark stood at the end of the bed so the older man could see him without moving. His respect for old Bob grew almost to rival his admiration for Sally, and in a way there was something more compelling in his feelings for the older man than for the daughter.

Lambert had spent a lifetime building and carving and holding his ranch. It was a labor of love that had taken its toll in sweat and years, and now he had to lie there, waiting for an agonizing end before he cashed in. He had to live with the knowledge that his empire would crumble with his passing, because he had no one but a girl to leave it to. Mark Webb knew these things because he, too, was working toward a spread of his own, and the certain knowledge of the tribulations and sorrows that beset a rancher were imbedded in him.

"Bob, the coyote who knocked you over was a Mex." He held up the Mauser cartridge. "We don't use Mausers this side of the border."

Lambert's eyes were a little bitter and wholly indifferent. "It don't make much difference any more, Mark. I'll never get up again, so revenge won't do me any good." The direct blue eyes stared up at the blank ceiling. "When a man's got to stare at a damned ceiling all day long an' most o' the night, he gets to look at things differently. Don't bother huntin' that bushwhackin' *hombre*, Mark. Whether he's ever caught or not won't change things for the Rafter L." The large eyes slid down to Mark's face with a frank plea in their depths. "Just do me one favor, will you?"

Mark nodded soberly.

"Stay with Sally until the ranch is goin' real good . . . At least till after roundup, so's she can depend on someone. Will you?"

"You got my word for it, Bob." Mark left the room abruptly. He wasn't being rude, but there was something burning behind his eyes that demanded cool night air. He walked out into the ranch yard and looked up at the brilliant, brittle stars that shone down curiously on the quiet, brooding Rafter L. He didn't even turn when he heard footsteps that stopped beside him.

"What's the matter, Mark?"

He just shook his head and stared straight ahead. The distant, eerie cry of a coyote came down the mysterious night air and Sally looked up anxiously.

"Mark. You're not leaving?" Her voice was higher than usual and with a hint of a tremor in it.

He swung around savagely, his face pale and drawn in the ghostly light. "No, Sally. I'll leave when I've finished two jobs here."

"What are they?"

"Gotten the Rafter L through its roundup, an' found me a bushwhacker!"

Mark was pushing cattle back away from the border when two strangers rode slowly up to the Rafter L ranch house and asked for him. Sally showed them where to put their horses and made them a lunch while they waited. There was a little uneasiness in the pit of her stomach as she studied the men. Their clothing indicated a long, weary ride. One of them was cold-eyed, quiet, and wore two tied-down guns, the other, an older man, looked like a drummer.

When she led up indirectly to their business with Mark, they just smiled evasively and turned the subject to general topics. By the time Webb rode in, Sally was afraid. She met Mark at the corrals as he unsaddled and turned his horse loose and, fingers entwined, eyes large and worried, told him about the two strangers.

Mark listened calmly, flung his saddle over a pole on the top of the corral, and looked down into her eyes. Something shattered his control then; perhaps it was the appealingly helpless and loyal look on her face. His grin sobered as he leaned against the corral, one arm still resting lightly across the saddle. "Sally, did anyone ever tell you you're beautiful?"

She was startled and showed it.

Mark took the arm from across the saddle and shoved both hands into his Levi's pockets. He was as red as a beet. "I'm sorry." There was a tumult of words in his throat but he couldn't express them sensibly, so he started for the house.

Sally stood perfectly still and looked at him as he swung past. "Mark."

He stopped and turned, eyes smoky and ashamed. "Yes?"

"What about the two men in the house?"

He shrugged. "They're friends of mine . . . that letter you mailed for me brought 'em here."

He started to turn again when she walked a little closer to him and spoke: "In that case, then I'll answer your other question. Yes, I've been told that before, but I've never particularly wanted to hear it . . . before."

Mark didn't know what to say, so he just looked at her and the mantle of red faded a little as they stood, looking at one another. Sally smiled and Mark's courage came back in a rush.

"In that case I'll say something else, and then you can fire me." He shoved his hands deeper into his pockets and seemed to brace his shoulders. "I'm in love with you, Sally." He saw the startled look reappear and his own words sounded terribly blunt and crude to him so he talked on, trying to soften them. "I've known it since the day I met you on the trail an' you sent me after Parson Rigby. It's crazy an' I know it, but anyway, Sally, there it is." His eyes swept up and rested on hers. "Now you can fire me."

Sally saw the very self-conscious little grin on his face and she smiled. "Don't be sorry, Mark. I wouldn't fire you, anyway. Will you do me a favor?"

"Sure, name it."

Her eyes were moist and her breathing came in fluttering little breaths from between her open lips. There was a mischievous twinkle in her eyes, along with a lot of tenderness. "Go in the house and see your friends."

Mark watched her turn, walk to the corral, and lean against it. He understood instinctively that she wanted to be alone. He hesitated, then swung around and headed for the house. For some inexplicable reason he felt guilty and ashamed.

CHAPTER
FOUR

When Mark entered the Rafter L living room, two sets of quizzical, affable eyes were watching him. The man with the two guns got up casually and walked over to him with an outstretched hand.

"Mark, when you talk to real pretty women, you'd oughta know better than to do it where folks can see you from the window."

Webb avoided the kidding face, but shook the hand. "Y'damned nosy ol' dog. A man's got a right to . . ."

The well-fed, professional-looking man laughed and got up with an outstretched hand. "Listen, Son, it's about time you settled down."

Mark's face was red again and he grinningly, guiltily, motioned toward chairs. "Look, you chuckwallas, I didn't get you down here to spy on me. I got a story to tell you."

It didn't take long for Mark Webb to tell the strangers all he knew about Lambert's attempted murder and the state of the Rafter L.

When he was finished, the older man got up. "All right, Son, where's the wounded man?"

Mark led the way to Lambert's room, peeked in, got a gruff invitation to enter, and the three men walked to the foot of the bed.

Mark looked down at Bob Lambert. "Bob, I hope you don't get sore about it, but I've gone an' called my dad to come down here an' look at you." He put a lean, bronzed hand on the heavy-set man's shoulders. "This is my father, Doctor Samuel Webb, of Nogales, an' I thought he might be able to look you over."

Bob Lambert's eyes were startled as they surveyed the capable-looking man, and then swung to the hard-eyed, silent man next to him. Mark saw Lambert's eye appraise the other man. "This is my brother, Cal. I sort of figured he could help me around the ranch for a while."

There was a long moment of quiet before Bob Lambert's eyes, blinking fast, turned back to Mark. "Dammit, you hadn't oughta made them ride all the way down here." It wasn't exactly a reproof, but old Bob felt he had to say something gruff; it was his way.

Dr. Webb nodded tolerantly and moved around to the side of the bed with the assurance of perfect confidence in himself. He stopped and looked at his two sons. "Suppose you boys go rope a cow, or ride a horse, or something, for a while, and send that young lady in here to me."

Mark and Cal nodded and went out. They met Sally coming in and Mark introduced his brother, who managed a wide-eyed and gulping: "Proud to know you, ma'am."

"Sally, my father's in with Bob an' he wants you to come in. He's a doctor, Sally." He hesitated, wanted to say something else, felt Cal's eyes on him, and smiled instead as he went on out of the house followed by his brother.

26

"Lord, Mark, who'd ever have thought there was anything like that 'way out here?" Cal's face was smothered in a look of rapture. "Man, did you ever see anything like her? *¡Hijo de puta!* She's —"

"Aw, shut up. I didn't get you down here to listen to your palaver." He fished the brass cartridge case out of his shirt pocket. "See that?"

Cal Webb took it and turned it over carefully as he studied it. "Yeah."

"I found it in the rocks where Lambert was shot."

Cal nodded slowly. "Mex shell. Out of a Mauser."

"That's the way I figure it. Of course, it don't help much, but at least we're pretty sure it was a Mex that plugged him."

Cal returned the shell case. "That all you got to go on?"

Mark sank into a chair on the verandah and his brother sat down next to him. "Yep, that's the whole case, so far." He began to roll a cigarette. "What d'ya reckon we ought to do now?"

Cal shrugged. "There's not much we can do. We can't go into Mexico an' round up every Mex packin' a Mauser. Hell, they all got 'em. That's standard *revolucionista* equipment down there." He relaxed and looked out over the peaceful landscape. "We can nose around a little, but actually there's nothin' much we can do right off, anyway."

At dinner, that evening, Mark never saw Sally so radiant. Her eyes sparkled, and the lantern light cast shimmering flecks of pure gold from the sheen of her hair. Mark and Dr. Webb watched in high amusement as Cal stumblingly helped with the cooking, the table setting, and the serving. There was a lump in Mark's throat every time his eyes crossed with Sally's. His father knew this, too; his diagnosis of the Rafter L, in general, was acutely correct and precise. He hadn't missed a thing. In fact, he knew something Mark would have given his right arm to know.

When Mark met Sally, as he and Cal were saddling up to ride over the Rafter L, he asked her about her father.

Sally's face was solemnly grateful. "You father said that Dad should've had efficient medical help at the first . . . but that, even so, the operation is comparatively simple. He's sure Dad'll be up and around in six months." The tears started then and she practically fell into Mark's arms. "Oh, Mark, how can I ever thank you? I'm so grateful." Her body shook in tight sobs and Mark forgot that Cal was standing, open-mouthed, a few feet away.

"I don't want gratitude, Sally. I'd have done as much for anyone."

Her tear-stained face came up, and Cal ran a tender, caressing arm around the indifferent neck of his blocky bay horse as Mark's face went down and their lips met. The bay horse lay back his ears and darted a quick nip at Cal and the cowboy looked up, startled, to see that he had a handful of neck skin in his fist. He let go quickly, coughed loudly, and swung up on the horse.

★ ★ ★

"Oh, Lord" — Cal was rocking ecstatically in his saddle — "I don't want gratitude!" Mark was uncomfortably miserable and red-faced. "Oh, not that line, Mark." He leaned toward his brother with a wide-eyed look on his face. "Back in Nogales I learned to say that in two languages, an' never got to first base. Look, *hombre*, use a different approach. Say —"

"Shut up, you loud-mouthed sump hole. Dammit, you shouldn't have even been there."

Cal put up a protesting hand and a look of indignation swept over him. "Not been there? Hell, I have no way of knowin' when some lovesick renegade's goin' to come loose at the seams an' start kissin' people. My gosh, man, can't you give a feller a little warnin', like maybe shootin' off your gun, or havin' a fit, or somethin'?"

Mark's embarrassed eyes swept the horizon unseeingly, widened, swung back, and lost their unhappy discomfort. He reined up suddenly and pointed ahead. Cal, mouth still opened in protest, stopped and looked in the direction of his brother's arm. "What's that?"

Cal's face sobered in an instant. "Looks like three *hombres* drivin' some cattle." They sat still and watched the advancing cattle with three riders flanking them. The drive would come right past them, so they sat still and studied the scene. Cal's frown was intent.

"Thought you said this was all Rafter L range an' there were no steady Rafter L riders?"

Mark nodded. "I did. We got no hired hands an' this is all Rafter L range. Deeded range, in fact, an' no one's got a right to cross it without permission." The cattle were closer now and they were veering off a little from the motionless riders. Mark frowned. "Hell, those're Rafter L cattle."

Cal looked at the large "Rafter L" branded on the right ribs of the critters, then his curious gaze lifted to the riders. Two were Mexicans and one was an American. The riders swerved off their course and approached the Webb brothers. Mark stole a quick look at Cal, whose relaxed figure was intent on the oncoming cowboys.

"Howdy."

"Howdy."

"You *hombres* work for the Rafter L?"

Mark nodded his head. The Mexicans were both dark, wiry men with blank faces, booted carbines, and six-shooters hanging from cartridge belts that also supported knives. They rode American stock saddles, though, and had manila ropes instead of their own native rawhide reatas. The American was badly pockmarked, thick-shouldered, with brittle, gray eyes, a thin, petulant mouth, and two tied-down guns, plus his Winchester .30-30 carbine. Mark's eyes swung avidly to the Mexicans' rifle boots, but all he could see were the butt plates, not enough to see whether the men had Mausers or not.

"Well, we picked up this little bunch of Rafter L cattle just over the line an' thought we'd bring 'em back to you."

Mark nodded agreeably. "That was right decent of you."

The American shrugged. "Oh, it war'n't nothin'. We was comin' over anyway." He let his eyes slide from Cal to Mark. "They's another bunch of them where those come from, but they're in good feed an' we'll drive 'em back in a few days when we come back again."

Mark was mildly puzzled. "Tell us where they are, an' we'll go get 'em. No sense in you havin' to do our work."

The American smiled and shrugged. "Hell, we got business up here anyway, an', besides, we know how to get 'em across without a lot of damn' fool questions bein' asked." He winked meaningly. "Don't bother about 'em. We'll push 'em across in two, three days."

Cal and Mark thanked the men, offered to pay them, which was laughingly turned down, took over the cattle, and began the drive to the Rafter L corrals after waving casually to the departing American and his two pokerfaced helpers.

CHAPTER
FIVE

Mark swung off his horse and slammed the corral gate behind the cattle as Cal pushed the last dogie through. They stood in silence, looking at the animals.

"It could've happened that they drifted below the border, Cal. There hasn't been a steady rider on the Rafter L since Bob got shot, an' Sally's had to stay pretty close to her dad most of the time . . . so it's possible they just strayed over there."

Cal nodded and began slowly to roll a cigarette. "Yeah, it makes sense, all right. But what doesn't make sense . . . to me, anyway . . . is why those shady-lookin' *hombres* would bring back such slick, fat cattle when they could 'a' sold them below the line for a damned good price."

Mark shrugged. "You're always figurin' every down-at-the-heel 'puncher is an owl-hooter. Hell, they're probably just as honest as anyone in Lodgepole."

Cal lit the cigarette and answered wryly. "That ain't sayin' much, from what I saw of Lodgepole when we rode through it."

Mark was turning toward Cal to vent a little irritation, when one of the cows in the corral caught his eye. He studied her for a moment, but she pushed in among the other animals, and he clambered up the corral and perched on the top pole with a suddenly intent glint in his eye.

"Come on up here a minute, Cal."

Mark's brother heaved himself up. "Well? Do they look better when you're lookin' down on 'em?"

Mark's eyes flickered from one animal to another. He saw it again, and again — always in the same place, too. He jumped down and grabbed his saddle horn, swung aboard, and took down his rope. "Come on, Cal. We're goin' to stretch one out."

Cal grumblingly clambered down off the corral and opened the gate to let Mark through and led his own horse inside before he slid the gate latch bar back into place. The cows were pushed into an adjoining pen. Mark darted over to the next corral and slammed the gate, leaving one wild-eyed critter inside with him. Cal was mounted, with a long loop draped over his shoulder, watching his brother's antics with a puzzled frown.

"Just what in hell's wrong with you?"

Mark ignored the question. "You want to head or heel?" Cal shrugged and nudged his horse a little closer. Mark quartered the cow, and she moved away from the fence. Instantly his loop settled around her neck. She bellowed once and plunged, red-eyed, with saliva dripping from her mouth. Cal watched his chance, flicked his rope, flipped his slack while his horse was backing. Before she knew it, the cow was flat on her side. Mark dismounted, forced enough slack to shove one of her front hoofs through the strangling rope around her neck, thus assuring her enough rope tolerance to breathe, pushed back his Stetson, and motioned to Cal.

"I was right. Come here an' look at this."

Cal dismounted and came forward, still wearing the puzzled look. The men squatted by the cow and Mark ran a hand over the long, shaggy white coat of her belly. He pushed back the hair and disclosed a raw-looking gash. Dried blood was sticking to the hair, but even so the men found several crude stitch marks. Mark sat back triumphantly on his spurs and looked at his brother.

"Well, Brains, give me the answer to that."

Cal ignored Mark and probed the wound carefully with drawn eyebrows. He swung away from the cow and looked into the adjoining corral. "They all got it, by gosh. But you gotta be on your nose in the dirt to see it."

Mark nodded. "That's right. Now what in hell's it mean?"

Cal got up slowly. "Turn her loose." They went back to their horses and worked the critter loose. She leaped to her feet, trembling, and they let her in with the others. She forced her way deeply into the mass of dark red bodies and the two brothers unsaddled and turned their riding stock loose in a horse corral.

"Got it figured out yet?"

Cal sank down on the cracked and bleached mending bench outside the barn. He shook his head as Mark rolled a cigarette.

"Well, I have."

"All right, Casanova, let's have it."

Mark puffed slowly, abstractedly on the cigarette. "The way I got it figured, somebody drove those cattle over the line, slit their hides open, stuck something in there like dope or gold, patched 'em up again an' drove 'em back over the line without arousing any interest, then opened 'em up on this side, took out whatever they'd sewed in, and brought 'em on home."

Cal appropriated his brother's tobacco sack as it was disappearing into Mark's shirt pocket and rolled a cigarette. "Lord, what a trick. You s'pose that's it?" He nodded slowly before Mark could answer. "That'd account for how the contraband gold gets into the country all right, at that." He nodded his head. "Clever, dammit. Damned clever."

Mark smoked slowly and his eyes were squinted. "Cal, it all fits together now. Listen, see how it sounds to you. Bob Lambert's constant ridin' was keepin' his cattle away from where the renegades could drive off a few head an', besides, him bein' abroad all the time made it hard for 'em to hold and work the critters once they were across the line, so they blasted him. After that, they had it all their way. No interference, no trouble gettin' Rafter L cattle that they'd return every now an' then, and a nice quiet length of border where it was pretty safe to operate."

Cal turned at the sound of footsteps and hastily doffed his hat as he arose, speaking quietly out of the corner of his mouth. "Here comes the future Missus Webb. You got it figured about right, but don't tell anybody on the Rafter L. This is our little secret."

Sally smiled uncertainly. "Am I interrupting something?"

Cal shook his head with elaborate slowness. "No, ma'am. Nothing that won't keep. I'll go up to the house an' see how Dad's makin' out with his patient. See y'all later." Mark wanted to laugh at the way his brother got out of there.

"Sit down, Sally."

"What're you two conspirators up to, Mark?"

He shrugged casually. "Nothin' much. We just corralled a bunch of Rafter L critters some riders said they'd pushed out of Mexico."

Sally smiled. "I know. I saw you and your brother corralling them."

Mark changed the subject abruptly. "How's Bob?"

"All worked up. Doctor Webb says we'll get Parson Rigby tomorrow, and, by using him, instead of either one of you, we'll operate on him."

Mark frowned slightly. "Sally, there's always a risk. I mean . . ."

"I know what you mean, Mark. Dad knows it, too, but he's awfully impatient to get on with it. He says he'd rather be dead all over than half dead." She looked down at her lap. "He's always been such an active man, Mark." Abruptly her head swung up and the faith and courage in her innocent eyes made Mark look away. "It'll come out all right, Mark, I know it will."

Mark and Cal rode after the parson and returned with him, left him with Sally at the ranch house, and rode quickly off across the Rafter L range. Cal was

36

muttering more to himself than his brother as they rode away.

"Never had no stomach for it, damned if I did."

Mark knew what he meant and remained silent. They scoured the range until they found what they were looking for, a torn-up, ragged section of ground where one man had held the stock off a ways, while two men roped and stretched them out in order to retrieve the contraband. They even found little hard cakes of dried blood. Cal was a little pale when he remounted.

"Cuttin' an' brandin' always makes me a little sick, but deliberately cuttin' under a critter's hide, sewin' somethin' into it, then openin' them again, makes me *real* sick."

Mark nodded. "A man that'd do that is worse than an animal."

Cal and Mark split up. Cal rode off, heading northwest, apparently in a hurry, while Mark appeared to be making a more leisurely survey of the Rafter L property line which, naturally, ran only as far as the national boundary line. The brothers had held a long talk before splitting up and the day was well spent before they met again at the corrals of the Rafter L. Mark appraised his brother as the latter was unsaddling. Cal had the whitish, powdery dust on him that was indigenous to the country around Lodgepole.

"Well, how'd it come out?"

Cal slung his saddle on the corral rail and grunted with the effort. "All right. Just as we figured it should. How's Lambert?"

Mark turned toward the house. "Don't know. I haven't been up there yet. Come on."

Parson Rigby met them in the living room. He was white-faced and tense. "That was an ordeal, gentlemen, that I'd not care to repeat."

Mark looked searchingly into the parson's face with a sinking feeling in his stomach. "How'd it come out?"

Rigby sank weakly into a chair and shook his head as he mopped at his forehead with a white handkerchief. "Oh, Bob's going to be all right, the doctor said so." He looked up suddenly, eyes pinioning Mark. "Why didn't you tell me?"

Mark shrugged. "Never had a chance. Besides, when we first met I didn't see . . ."

Rigby held up a hand. "Yes, I know, code of the West. None of my . . . ahem . . . darned business who your father was." He dabbed at his forehead again. "I see now why your father said you boys weren't any good at a thing like that. Neither am I."

Cal turned slowly when Sally entered the room. The strain had been a killing one and it showed. She was blank except for her large, direct eyes that, in the tight, blanched background of her face and the bloodless line of her mouth, looked twice as large and appealing. She sat down slowly and Cal put a clumsy, protecting arm across her shoulders. He knew he ought to say something, but he was tongue-tied, so he patted her gently, awkwardly.

On the Rafter L, probably the least affected were the patient, who slept deeply from the opiates, and the surgeon, who blandly went about cleaning instruments, a fragrant Havana cigar jutting rakishly from the corner of his mouth. It was Dr. Webb who finally raised the morale of the others sufficiently to warrant interest in dinner and, while Sally mechanically went about getting the meal, the parson excused himself and rode hastily back toward Lodgepole as soon as the first smell of frying meat assailed his nostrils.

It had been a trying day and the Rafter L slept soundly through the deep, velvety night, serenaded by the wise little prairie wolves that laughed at the moon and sang to one another across the broad sweep of the slumbering land.

CHAPTER
SIX

Cal and Mark left the Rafter L before the others were stirring. They had planned it that way. There were awkward questions they wanted to avoid answering, and, moreover, there was the possibility, since they knew practically nothing of the men they were after, that their calculations might go astray.

The sun was high when Mark rode back from the slight eminence of Tiburcio Rocks to Cal. He nodded brusquely. "It's workin', Cal. They're comin'. I could just barely make 'em out."

Cal smiled wolfishly, and the two men swung off across the range toward the border. They hadn't ridden a mile before they reined up and sat silently watching a repetition of the former cattle drive. The same three men were driving a small herd of Rafter L cattle back from below the border. As they swept in closer, Cal grunted: "The same *hombres*. Ol' Pock Face and his *cucarachas*."

Mark held up his hand, and the riders left their herd and came toward the brothers.

The venomous-looking *gringo* was smiling broadly. "It's jus' like I tol' ya. We brang 'em back." He shrugged casually. "We was crossin' through anyway, so, like I tol' ya, we really ain't puttin' oursel'es out none."

Mark grinned sardonically. "No, of course not. In fact, it'd be kind of unhandy for you to come across without bringin' the Rafter L cows back, wouldn't it?"

The renegade's face lost its triumphant smile. His eyes flickered between the two silent, watching cowboys before him and his tongue made a quick, darting circuit of his thin lips. "What ya mean, *hombre*?"

Cal spit disdainfully before he spoke. "A man that'd rip up a dumb critter's hide to conceal contraband so's he could sneak it across the border is just about the lowest specimen I can imagine."

The renegade's hands were resting lightly on the saddle horn. He was silent for a long moment before a blustering smile broke out over his features. "Aw, now, listen, boys, a man's got to make a livin', ya know." He motioned casually to the uneasy, drifting cattle. "After all, them cows ain't hurt much, an' besides what's it to you *hombres* anyway, them's Rafter L cattle, an' there ain't no call for a couple of hired riders to get proddy about it."

Cal's hand went up slowly and flipped up the flap of his shirt pocket. A glitter of morning sunlight flashed brilliantly off the little badge pinned there. The renegade didn't have to get any closer to see the lettering that said: UNITED STATES DEPUTY MARSHAL. He had seen more than one of those badges in his long, checkered, and unsavory career.

Mark knew it was coming and was braced, but even so it happened so fast he was almost caught off guard. The American renegade hadn't moved his hands. They still lay athwart the saddle horn while his wily eyes searched the two faces in front. It was one of the *cholos* who made the break, and that was the key for all of them to go into action. The Mexican yanked his six-gun out with more murderous fury than skill, but, since he was partially concealed from the Webbs by the American outlaw, Mark was two seconds behind in his own stab for a gun. The *cholo* was screaming curses and imprecations as he fired. The shot was close to Cal, but it missed. Mark's gun was in his hand as all hell broke loose.

Cal swung his horse sideways as the American renegade sank in his spurs, pulled a gun, leaped ahead, and fired, all at nearly the same time. The shot went wild but it served its purpose. The *gringo* was riding wide open across the range in a frantic bid for freedom. Cal cursed, yanked his horse around, and leaped out in savage pursuit. Mark fired twice more at the Mexican *alambrista* who had first opened hostilities. The man sat straight in his saddle, a look of amazement on his face. He swung his gun up again, looked wide-eyed at Mark, hesitated, then slumped forward, falling heavily, soddenly, off his snorting horse.

Mark was moving as he fired. He had odds of two to one, and, until he downed the first man, he didn't want to increase his danger by sitting still. When the first Mexican slid off his horse, the second one swore a violent Spanish oath, whirled his horse, and rode bent low over the animal's neck toward the border and safety.

Mark rocketed along, eyes squinted against the rush of cool morning air against his face. Occasionally the

Mexican would turn in his saddle and throw a wild shot at Mark in the desperate hope that it would slow down his pursuer, but Mark bored in, his horse slowly gaining on the mount of the fugitive, which had been used hard, roping cattle most of the night, and was tired and weary from work and sleeplessness.

What happened to Mark and his prey was wholly unexpected. The Mexican's horse stumbled, regained its footing, stumbled again and fell heavily on its side, catapulting its rider violently through the air. He struck the ground, rolled several times, and to Mark's everlasting amazement bounced to his feet, teeth bared, hair awry, and the powdery dust rising from him like steam, gun blazing.

Mark yanked back and slid off his horse, turning the animal sideways as he went. A bursting, red-hot blast of pain went through his right leg and the knee buckled as he hit the ground. Another bullet tore his Stetson from his head and sent it sailing like a frantic black bird off across the range. Mark was on one knee when he fired. The Mexican was spraddle-legged, teeth bared, his eyes wild and shiny. Mark thumbed two more shots and saw the Mexican stagger, weave slightly, and thumb his gun again. Mark felt the ghostly song of death as the renegade's bullet went closely past his face. He raised his gun carefully, unmindful of the Mexican's fire, aimed carefully, and was in the act of squeezing the trigger when the wobbly renegade caved in and fell flat on his face.

A gentle, sighing little stray zephyr picked the moment of silence after the wild gunfight to blow caressingly across the grass. Mark got painfully to his feet, holstered his gun, and slit the seam of his Levi's for a close inspection of his leg wound. The sticky warmth of his own blood was slippery where it ran down his leg into his boot. Apparently the renegade's bullet had missed the bone of his upper leg, but, judging from the agonizing sensations that permeated him when he probed it, the slug hadn't skirted many muscles or nerves. Relieved to see that the wound wasn't particularly dangerous, Mark grimaced wryly and hobbled toward the downed Mexican. He rolled the man over and studied him closely. There were two bullet holes in his body. One was low in the abdomen, which must have been the first to hit him, while the second was in the right side of his chest. The man was dead.

Mark was in the process of hobbling up to his snorting horse when Cal loped up. His face was damp with sweat and his eyes were slits. "Well, I see you got yours, too."

Mark climbed laboriously aboard his horse with clenched teeth. "You get the *gringo?*"

"I chased him right into the sheriff's arms. In a way it was sort of funny. After talkin' to the sheriff when I went to Lodgepole yesterday, the old boy must've gotten downright indignant that smugglers would use his territory for their labors. He was comin' across the range toward the Rafter L and this renegade smuggler was hightailin' it like a cut cat when the sheriff an' his posse loomed up. The posse just sort of fanned out an' closed in with this renegade in the middle. He was caught before he knew what it was all about."

The horses were moving slowly and each impact of a hoof on the hard ground sent a jolt of pain through Mark. Cal noticed the whiteness of his brother's face. "You hit?"

Mark nodded.

"Bad?"

"No, just a slug through the leg above the knee, but I've felt more like dancing in my life."

Cal frowned. "You ride on to the Rafter L an' I'll meet you there as soon as I check on the other one. The sheriff's there, waitin'."

Mark shook his head. "No, I'll go with you an' we'll both ride in later."

The first casualty of the brief, savage battle was still on the ground where he had fallen off his horse. He wasn't dead, but he wasn't effervescent with life, either. Cal hoisted him onto his own horse like a sack of flour, tied him securely, and the men rode on to the Rafter L buildings where they turned their prisoner over to the sheriff's posse. Sally and Dr. Webb literally swept Mark into the house, under his expressions of mild resentment and irritation, while Cal and Sheriff Molden from Lodgepole talked in the warm, sunlighted yard before the old house.

"Hell, Marshal, why didn't you check in at the office when you come through Lodgepole? I'd've been plumb glad to work with you."

Cal smiled affably and shoved his Stetson to the back of his head. "To tell you the truth, Sheriff, I had no idea it was a federal job when I came down here from Nogales. All I knew was that my brother, Mark, wrote me to come on down an' bring our father, and that a man he was workin' for had been mysteriously shot." He shrugged his broad shoulders. "I didn't know there was anything really wrong until the evenin' before I rode in to talk with you. In fact, no one knew I was a deputy U.S. marshal until these here smugglers showed up."

Molden looked at the sulking, cowering American renegade where he stood with the posse. "Hey, *hombre*. Which one o' you shot Bob Lambert?"

The evil, dissolute face came up and the baleful eyes swung to the wounded Mexican tied across the horse. "That damned fool there. His name's Sence Pastor."

The sheriff stuck out his hand. "Well, Marshal, reckon I'd better get back to town with these two. Stop in the next time you're in town."

Cal assured him he would as he watched the posse ride away, then he turned slowly and went up to the house. There was a low rumble of voices as Cal entered the living room. Mark was explaining to Sally why he hadn't mentioned the fact that his brother was a deputy U.S. marshal, and Sally was sitting close to the bandaged leg, listening. Cal cleared his throat, and Sally turned.

"What's the matter, Cal? Have a cold?"

Cal shook his head carefully. "No, but every once in a while folks forget I'm around and . . ."

Mark snorted. "Aw, shuddup." His voice was full of disgust. "Just 'cause a man kisses his future wife once . . ."

46

"Oh, so it's a future wife now, is it?"

Sally was reddening and Mark squirmed comfortably. "Well, what's wrong with gettin' married, anyway?"

Cal shrugged as he moved toward Bob Lambert's room where two voices came faintly to him as Dr. Webb and his patient hashed over the unexpected happenings of the day. "Nothin'. Nothin' at all. In fact, people are doin' it every day or so. But in your letter you said you wanted to clear up this mess for the sake of vengeance alone against the men that shot Lambert." Again the shrug. "Sure's a funny way to get revenge, marryin' a man's daughter."

Sally was smiling through her embarrassment and Mark was glowering. "Aw shuddup, ya flannel mouth."

GUNS
IN
OREGON

CHAPTER
ONE

In moonlight the town appeared as an improbable dream because all around it lay forests and peaks and undergrowth as tall as a man, except right where the town sat, and there, in a clearing of perhaps a hundred acres, lay the town of Younger. Daylight, though, made a difference, for the village wasn't all that isolated. The forests remained, but southerly and westerly they were much thinner, permitting sunlight to reach the ground, and there, for miles and miles as far as a man could see, was grassland. There were also creeks foaming down out of the northward mountains. It was a good country for livestock. For horses and horned cattle — but not for sheep because those northward ranges showed in their dark brooding that they concealed cougars and wolves and coyotes, varmints who lived off sheep if they ever got a chance.

Just north of Younger an old duffer had once brought in a few woollies. He was out of business in something like fifteen days. No one else ever emulated him, but the chances for this ever becoming sheep country were slight even without the catamounts. High desert wasn't a desert at all; it had once put some long-ago trappers in mind of the desert because it was an immense plateau, and they'd hit it in summertime when it was very hot and sultry, and also right after some bands of withdrawing Nez Percés had set fire to the underbrush to keep the ground clean. Of course, the trees had been burnt, too, but that had been a lifetime or more ago, the trees had returned a dozen fold, grass took over from the defunct brush, and the high desert was as lush and desirable a country for livestock as a man ever set eyes upon.

Still, the town of Younger was isolated. A weekly coach went through but generally all it brought south from Salem was the mail, rarely a passenger, and rarer still, an outsider who deliberately journeyed to Younger to stay. That was, indeed, a *very rare* occurrence. Unless a person had specific business in Younger, there wasn't any point in going there. There was a livery barn, an apothecary's shop, the inevitable gun shop and harness works, two log saloons, a bakery, a big general mercantile establishment — whose inventory was as varied as any in Oregon — and some other lesser places of business such as cafés and a laundry and a deputy sheriff's office. But there was no hotel. Visitors, when they came, had to hope that Mrs. Beeman's boarding house had a vacancy or — as Agatha Beeman called it — "an empty".

But the village of Younger was far from being a dull or colorless place. Southward and westward lay the cow outfits. Mostly these were ranches controlling in excess of 10,000 acres. Three or four of them ran cattle all the way north to the Cascades, or as far south as The Dalles. There were innumerable line camps — isolated log cabins with perhaps a small corral — scattered throughout this grasslands country where riders could bed down, or for that matter, if hunting cattle, could stay for a week or two while riding a particular area of the ranges. It was these rugged men that kept Younger from ever getting too drowsy or lethargic, particularly if they'd been out a few weeks at the line shacks. Then they came to town bubbling with ferment, and it paid folks to step a little lightly.

These men came from everywhere. There were Montanans, Coloradoans, Mormon cowboys from over in Utah, and innumerable riders from the parched Southwest. It was these Southwesterners who could ride better, rope better, shoot straighter, and howl louder. There were also Texans, a scattering of boys from Indian Territory, that lay northward from Texas, and now and then one ran across the flat accent of the Nebraska or Kansas plains, or even the slow, slurred drawl of Arkansas. Cowboys invariably, wherever one encountered them, were from anywhere and everywhere. In Oregon not many were natives, but then not many of the big cowmen were natives, either, because Oregon was just too big and too new to have many natives who didn't sport feathers in their hair. Charley Deems who operated the general store in Younger called the native Indians "smoked Irishmen". Charley, though, was a dehydrated dollar chaser who had a sort of sneer for everyone, unless they happened to have as much money as he did, or perhaps more money; then Charley was courteous. He didn't like many people, but that was somewhat equalized by the fact that not many people liked Charley. Still, in order to give the devil his due, Charley, barring his idiosyncrasies, wasn't a bad feller.

He'd been known to extend credit to more than one pilgrim from whom he knew — as well as everyone else knew — he'd never recover a red cent.

That was one thing about a place like Younger; it was isolated enough and insular enough so that everyone knew everyone else's business. Deputy Sheriff Jim Crawford said once that the best way to keep a secret in Younger was to rush right out and tell it first because, if you held off a few hours, everyone would find it out anyway, which was not altogether an exaggeration.

Generally, though, the people of the town weren't malicious. They gossiped, but slyly, and they were willing listeners to such juicy morsels of news as Cuff Banning's torrid affair with that red-headed girl who sang up at Bill Haines's Territorial Saloon. But that was primarily because they got so little news from the outside world. Oregon was as far across the North American land mass from the astringent Eastern seaboard as a man could get, unless he wanted to go wading. In fact, years before when the War Between the States had ripped the soft underbelly of the nation, the folks of Oregon in general and Younger in particular didn't even know war had come, until after nearly 100,000 battlefield casualties had been counted. Conversely, that war had been over six months before the officials of the state had stopped recruiting. Time, folks said philosophically — and without any real interest — would rectify that, but time never had. A generation had come to manhood since that war and Younger still was getting just one stage a week, freighters came in with supplies only during the summer — winters were too wet — and the last dot on the Western Telegraph Company's map of projected future expansion was Younger, Oregon.

That's why strangers arriving on the coach were sources of endless speculation and inquiry. If they came carrying saddles, they were naturally of less direct interest, for cowboys frequently arrived like that, and, since the demand for good riders was a constant thing, the Territorial Saloon, clearing house for all ranching proclivities, usually sent these men to some ranch the same day they hit town. But the afternoon of the midweek day that the stage brought Edward Given to Younger — without any saddle but dressed and armed like a range rider — things were different. For one thing Edward Given didn't fit the common description of a cowboy. He had a sprinkling of gray over the ears, was quiet, unassuming, asked no questions about jobs or anything else, and he did an unprecedented thing in a place where men were close with their funds. He didn't buy a five-cent shot of mountain dew up at the Territorial, he bought a full quart — and paid cash for it. He sampled the stuff, gravely wrote his name across the label, had a few more drinks, and told the barman to put it back on the shelf and thereafter, when he came in, to give him drinks from his own bottle. This was something entirely new and unheard of in Younger.

He got a room from Agatha Beeman, too, who afterward reported that Edward Given had a name — faithfully inscribed in her register — and he was a very mannerly gentleman. Agatha, a widow since her twenty-ninth year, was a little inclined to view single men with restraint but undeniable interest. In Given's case it was understandable. He was not a tall man — in his boots he stood no more than five feet eight or nine inches — but he had a certain grace to his movements that could mean a lot, or it could mean nothing except that he was especially well co-ordinated. His neck and head were the same size; his shoulders and arms were thick and powerful. His chest was heavy, but from there on down he tapered to a boyish leanness. He obviously was a man endowed by Nature with all the physical strength and stamina he'd ever need.

His features were good, although he seemed to have forgotten how to smile. His eyes gave the distinct impression that, without moving, they missed nothing. He was quiet to the point of taciturnity and made no attempt to cultivate friends, which perhaps more than anything else drove the folks of Younger to their wits' end — in some cases not a very long drive.

Bill Haines of the Territorial Saloon, a rugged old Missourian in Oregon for reasons he kept strictly to himself and who was a good judge of men, made only one appraisal of Edward Given: "A good feller to leave alone." Charley Deems had a more pointed observation. Charley curled his lip into its customary faint sneer and said: "He's a wanted man or I never saw one. Look how he wears that gun tied down in its cut-away holster."

Deputy Jim Crawford, a lanky Arkansan who carried a knife in his boot as well as a Derringer in his vest pocket, along with the customary .45 on his hip, was more charitable. But Jim was a feller who rarely said what he was privately thinking. The only observation he had to make was a drawled comment that if Given left Younger alone, Younger would leave Given alone.

And that's how things stood the first six days Edward Given was in town. It was on the seventh day things broke loose, and it happened down in front of Cliffy Hart's livery barn. Old Cliffy was the town character. It wasn't unusual for old Cliffy to show up with unmatched shoes on, or wearing a coat in mid-August. Some hinted that Cliffy wasn't quite all right upstairs, but not everyone believed that. Cliffy was eccentric, sure, but he ran a good barn, kept his horses in fine shape, and was quick to give anyone hell who brought in a sweaty animal. Also, he had money, which was Bill Haines's criteria.

"If a man can make a decent dollar in a place like Younger, then by grab he's not an idiot. You can take my word for *that!*"

This edict by Bill made sound sense; besides, Haines was respected in the Younger country. He'd proved himself a right stout man with his fists more than once, had never been known to dun anyone for bar accounts, and could be relied upon if an emergency arose in town. Bill Haines was the unofficial mayor of Younger just as Cliffy Hart was the unofficial town clown.

Cliffy had been an Indian fighter, an Army scout, a gold prospector in southern Oregon, and, some said, an unhung horse thief out in New Mexico, which was the reason he'd initially come on a fast animal up into the high desert country. He was crowding sixty, had hair as white as Mount Hood's snowcap, was as

57

thinned down and wiry as a hungry muskrat, stood about six feet tall when he stood straight — which he rarely did — and his pale blue eyes jumped around like a pair of rubber balls. He didn't seem capable of looking straight at anything — man or animal or scenery — for more than a moment or two at a time. He was outspoken and sometimes shrill. He was notoriously irascible and might explode any time he felt the slightest bit indignant. The people in town who knew Cliffy generally liked him. They didn't always agree with him and more often than not they laughed at his logic, but they liked him because old Cliffy Hart liked them.

He lived in a shack out behind the livery barn, never spoke of himself, his past, or even of his present, which was all right because Bill Haines and others never mentioned their pasts, either. It was one of the unwritten rules of the high desert that, unless a man first brought up the subject of his past, folks just didn't pry.

That story about Cliffy being an unhung horse thief had settled in the town some years earlier when a traveling drummer had gotten a good look at Cliffy Hart and had afterward said he'd known him over in Kansas years before, when old Cliffy had been a wanted man — a horse thief. No one ever repeated that story to Cliffy, naturally, and the peddler had gone on south with the stage, leaving behind his scurrilous saga. Whether it was true or not, one thing was very apparent: Cliffy knew horses and he loved them. Of course, that didn't necessarily make him a horse thief — lots of men loved horses — but it helped.

Until the arrival of Edward Given in Younger, no one knew something else about old Cliffy: he was a crack shot with a .45. That, of course, came not only as a total surprise, it also lent substance to that other yarn, for obviously while not all crack shots were horse thieves, if a man *was* a horse thief, being a marksman with a pistol sure helped him stay alive.

CHAPTER
TWO

It was a warm Thursday with springtime passing and summer beginning to increase its dehydrating hold on the countryside. Given had rented a top buggy from Cliffy and had gone out over the countryside. He hadn't said where he was going or why, and Cliffy hadn't asked, but in the afternoon, when Edward Given returned to town, two Swallowtail Ranch cowboys were out in front of the barn, along with a pair of riders from Cuff Banning's outfit, goading two shock-headed town kids into a fistfight. The riders had been drinking and the lads they were setting against one another weren't very well matched. In fact, one of them didn't weigh more than 130 pounds and every rib showed through his ragged, old, soiled shirt, while the other boy, easily forty pounds heavier and obviously a bully, was padded with muscle and without any question knew how to fight. It was this one who said, just as Cliffy and Edward Given walked up out of the barn's interior, that he'd clean the lighter lad's plow for half a silver dollar. This brought derisive laughter from Banning's men, who accused the Swallowtail men of putting their boy up to that. When this was denied, the coarse-featured, heavier lad, with a good audience, said he'd whip the other boy for nothing, and started forward.

60

It wouldn't be much of a fight; the slighter of those boys put up his fisted hands, but he patently knew nothing of this kind of battling. His face was gray and his eyes were dark with apprehension. He seemed to know what to expect but made no move to retreat from this punishment.

That was when Given stopped it. He gazed over at the half-drunk Swallowtail riders and said: "You pair of scum." He didn't add a word to that, but he didn't have to. Even Banning's men straightened up and turned around. Given eyed them, too. "You want to fight," he said, "step out into the roadway and square off, you two against the other two."

One of the Swallowtail riders, quicker than the others to recover from this unexpected intrusion, said: "Shorty, maybe you'd like a split lip." This man dropped his right hand, which was a serious mistake. Before he'd quite touched the butt of his .45, he was peering down into the tilted barrel of Given's gun, and that took all the speculation, all the uncertainty out of the whole affair. A man only drew a gun when he meant to use it. This was no longer rough sport; it was now a matter of life and death.

"You two boys," said Given, "walk over and stand against the front of the barn." The lads obeyed instantly, all their earlier trepidation or willingness to do battle entirely gone, their eyes big, their mouths agape. "You four," said Given to the range men, "walk out to the center of the roadway." For a second longer the cowboys stared; this had happened too quickly, too entirely without provocation in their view. Given cocked his .45. There was no longer the slightest shred of doubt about his intentions. The men turned and shuffled out into the afternoon-lighted roadway and turned back.

"Drop the guns."

The riders obeyed without any hesitation. Four to one were good odds, normally, but not when someone had a cocked gun in his fist. Besides, that gun had come out of its holster faster than any man in Younger had ever seen a gun drawn before.

"Now, fight!"

The pair of Swallowtail cowboys looked at Cuff Banning's men. One of them spat on his hands, balled them into fists, and said: "Hell, why not." He was coldly smiling when he launched himself through the air at the nearest Swallowtail rider.

Old Cliffy stepped over to where the fascinated youths were standing. He was as enthralled as the boys were, also. He grunted and rolled and winced as though actually participating, out there. When a man went down, he swore at him, commanding him to get up and fight. Across the road at the Territorial Saloon someone carried word of a terrific brawl outside, and men rushed forth to stare. Up and down the roadway spectators came out of stores. One man even came from the tonsorial parlor with the protesting barber right behind.

It was an excellent fight. If it hadn't commenced as one, after a few stinging blows had fallen on both sides, the battlers, already fired up on Bill Haines's potent whiskey, ignored Given with his cocked .45 and went to work with vigor. It culminated, though, when Deputy Crawford came out of his office, took one look, and rushed up the roadway to restore peace and order, not exactly the safest undertaking Crawford had ever embarked upon because by that time the Swallowtail men were fiercely abusing Banning's riders with epithets that heightened the ardor of the latter, which was in turn vented upon the former. But Jim Crawford was an Arkansas lad; he'd been taking care of himself in roadway brawls since he'd been big enough to bounce back up after being knocked down.

Crawford came upon the Swallowtail riders from behind, not really sporting, but then Jim wasn't out there to be sporting. He collared them both and heaved. The men went down in a howl of indignation from the bystanders up in front of Haines's place. To those men this was something no one had any right to interfere in. Among those protesting men was the Swallowtail Ranch foreman, Colin O'Brien, no mean fighter himself. He stepped down and started ahead just as Deputy Crawford drew his six-gun, pushed into the faces of Banning's boys, and swore a bleak oath. By the time O'Brien got out there, it was all over. He and Jim Crawford exchanged a hard look. There'd never been much affection between them anyway.

Crawford said, in that nasal drawl of his: "Well, you fixin' to buy in, too, Colin? Go ahead an' reach for that gun you're wearin'."

But Colin O'Brien was no fool. All he said was: "What's the matter with the boys havin' a little fun? You always got to go runnin' around being a killjoy, Jim?"

63

Crawford stepped back and put up his gun. "Get up," he said to the Swallowtail riders. "Who started this an' what was it about?"

The cowboys got up and started punching shirttails back into trousers, gingerly probing tender jaws, scooping up hats and guns, and glaring at each other, but they made no attempt at all to answer Crawford's question, and with good reasons; bad enough to get badgered into doing something as pointless and silly as this, but it would make each of them a laughing stock if word spread how one man — and shorter in stature than any of them, too — had gotten the drop on four range riders at once. No, they had nothing to say. They turned without another glance over to where Edward Given stood with those two boys and old Cliffy, and stalked on over to the saloon leaving O'Brien to face down Deputy Crawford.

"Well," the lawman demanded of Swallowtail's range boss. "What was it all about?"

"How the hell would I know?" growled O'Brien.

"You better know," snarled Crawford. "You're responsible for the boys you fetch into town from the ranch, an' you also know we don't stand for no brawlin' in Younger."

"Then sit for it," mumbled Colin O'Brien, and would have turned on his heel except that Edward Given strolled over and started to explain how it had all come about. O'Brien, like Jim Crawford, stood listening and making dour appraisals of the shorter, stockier man. When Given got to that part about getting the drop, Jim Crawford's face smoothed out in a thoughtful manner and his eyes drew narrow. O'Brien, though, snorted. He didn't believe any such ridiculous story.

"*You* got the drop on them *four?*" he said, curling his lip. "Don't hand me that, pilgrim. If that was wrote in a book, no one'd believe it even then."

Given put a long look over at Colin O'Brien. He seemed on the verge of saying something, then changed his mind and turned toward the deputy. "Do you know those two boys over in front of the livery barn?" he asked.

Jim looked. He knew them. The big, coarse-featured one was Bruce Horn, the blacksmith's son. The other one was an orphan who hung around town doing odd jobs.

"The big one was going to whip the other one," Given said. "That's why I stepped in. Wouldn't have been much of a scrap, Deputy."

Crawford privately agreed but he didn't say so aloud. All he said was: "Cliffy, did you see it start?"

Old Cliffy bobbed his head up and down, broadly grinning. "It happened just like Mister Given said, Jim. One of them Swallowtail men dived for his gun . . . and he never even got hold of it. If Colin don't believe it, I got an idea. Let Colin draw on Mister Given right now."

Jim Crawford growled at Cliffy about that. "You doggoned old coot, what you fixin' to do . . . get someone hurt?"

"Yeah," chuckled Cliffy. "Colin."

O'Brien was studying Edward Given now with a look of reluctant credibility. No man, O'Brien's common sense told him emphatically, was *that* fast with a gun.

Crawford said: "Go on, Colin. Go cool your head at the bar. And tell them rawhiders of yours the next time they set up a silly darned play like this, I'll lock 'em up until Christmas."

"You'll lock nobody up," growled O'Brien, who turned, and stalked back toward Haines's bar.

Crawford's lips were sucked back flat and he bored an unfriendly hole in Colin O'Brien's back as the range boss moved away.

Given said: "A regular holy terror, Deputy." He murmured it softly, also watching O'Brien. There was a strong leavening of quiet scorn in the statement.

Crawford turned and gave Given the same unfriendly look. "Mister, you better mind your manners in this town, and we got a real stout log jail house for troublemakers. As for *him*, nobody undersells Colin O'Brien. I've seen him eat up two your size before breakfast."

Crawford turned and walked back southward the way he'd come. Two things bothered him. Not the fight, actually, although it could possibly stir up bad blood between Cuff Banning's outfit and the Swallowtail. He'd cope with that, though, if it busted out in his township. He had the authority, and the ability as well, to break up dog fights. But there was the matter of how fast Given had drawn that gun. Cowboys were never good gunfighters; they rarely had time to practice shooting even, let alone drawing. And that probably meant that Jim Crawford had a damned gunslinger in his bailiwick.

The second worry Jim had was *why* a gunfighter would appear in an out-of-the-way hamlet like Younger. There were only two reasons gunfighters ever visited a town — to pass on through it, in which case they took the first stage out — or because they'd been hired and paid to come to a place and kill someone.

Well, he knew for a fact that Given had been in town a full week, which meant he wasn't just passing through, and which left the other ugly alternative. The hell of it was the law protected the innocent as well as the guilty. Jim couldn't order Given to ride on, or even lock him up for the protection of whomever he was here to liquidate, until Given broke a law, and with gunfighters, by the time the law was busted, the locking up was sort of anti-climatic. There was always a funeral *after* the locking up.

Jim went through his file of Reward posters. He even went through the ones stretching back over the tenure as local deputy of his predecessor — a man named Pyle who had died from close-range buckshot when he rode into an ambush set up for him by stage robbers.

There was nothing showing even a faint likeness to Edward Given. There were, on the other hand, among the posters lacking pictures at least fifty with a description that could have fitted Given. Jim gave up the search in disgust, sat down, and wrote out a minutely detailed description of his own, along with everything he knew or surmised, sealed it into an envelope, and put it in his pocket. He would give it to the northbound coach driver when the next stage came through, for delivery to the sheriff up at the county seat. The trouble with that, of course, was that, since the stage only passed through once a week, whatever Edward Given had in mind he'd probably accomplish and be gone long before the sheriff ever even saw Jim's letter.

That left Crawford with an obvious obligation. He would have to watch Given like a hawk. Would have to shadow him night and day. Fortunately Jim was a single man; more than one peace officer had lost a good woman because of inability to tell the truth convincingly about staying away from home all night. If Jim had other troubles, he at least didn't have that one.

There was one drawback, though, if Jim had to shag Given out over the range and be gone for long periods of time. The town would be left without adequate protection. If he appealed to the town council for the appointment of a temporary town marshal, and Given turned out not to be in Younger for purposes of assassination, Jim was going to be ragged to high heaven.

He decided in the end to say nothing to anyone, least of all the town council, until he heard from the sheriff or until Given gave him some more substantial reason to be suspicious. Then, he promised himself, he would arrest Given and lock him up.

With all that logically sorted out and decided upon, Crawford went along to supper. He also had a room at Agatha's place — was, in fact, Agatha's oldest steady boarder — and this gave him a fairly good position of observation over Edward Given.

The trouble was Edward Given didn't do a thing. He hired that orphan kid, whose name was Rusty Miller, to exercise his horse for an hour every day, and he frequently hired a rig and drove around the countryside, or took the kid to supper at Agatha's — paying extra, of course — or else he drank from his private stock over at the Territorial Saloon. Meanwhile, the stage came through, Jim gave the driver his letter to the sheriff surreptitiously, and instead of beginning to feel enormously relieved about his wasted time and evidently ill-founded suspicions respecting Given, it began to gnaw at Crawford that Given was just too cussed smooth for him. Given undoubtedly knew he was under close surveillance.

Bill Haines scoffed, when Jim finally hinted at his ideas regarding the stranger: "Hell," he gruffly said. "He's fast with a gun. What of it? He drinks like a gentleman, minds his business, and pays Agatha regular as clockwork. If that makes a feller a gunfighter, then maybe this town needs more of 'em."

CHAPTER
THREE

Then something happened that showed old Cliffy Hart to be a dead shot with a .45. It was in the morning when everyone had a perfect right to believe that the bland serenity of the overhead blue sky extended also to earth, and particularly to the village of Younger in Oregon. Moreover, hardly any trouble ever came much before five in the evening for the elementary fact that the ranch hands didn't much get off work before then to fog it on into town.

But this morning things were different. Possibly, had Arkansas Jim Crawford been more astute, or perhaps just older and more sagacious about such things, he'd have noticed that odd, green tint to the yonder foothills, or possibly the way Younger Creek over east of town was louder than it usually was. These were omens.

Another omen, more tangible and therefore more reliable, appeared when Colin O'Brien of the Swallowtail outfit rode into Younger escorting a ranch wagon. There were two cowboys on the seat of the rig but Colin was the only man among them a-horseback. It was unusual for a range boss to nursemaid two fully grown range riders into town. It was also unusual for all three of them to hit town so early in the day. Jim Crawford was still reading the mail up at his jail house office. Bill Haines was counting the silver in his safe up

70

at the Territorial Saloon. Charley Deems was leaning across his counter at the general store, studying a circular he'd gotten through the mail advertising some close-out supplies the Army wished to get rid of up at Steilacoom, and Edward Given was strolling from Agatha Beeman's place down toward the livery barn.

Cliffy saw Given coming and put aside his broom. He also saw that Swallowtail wagon up the northward road beyond Given but he paid no immediate attention to it because there were a few squatters over east of town clearing the forest from homesteaded land, and he thought, without looking closely, the wagon belonged to some of those callused, harmless, God-fearing folk.

Given was still 100 feet up the walk when old Cliffy recognized his mistake. That wasn't any sodbuster, that was the Swallowtail outfit, including Colin O'Brien, and, as Cliffy watched, Colin saw Edward Given walking along and drew up slightly in his saddle. Cliffy could almost feel Colin begin to bristle. Given still had no inkling of any undercurrent and, spying Cliffy in the livery barn doorway, paced along straight for him. He reached him, too, and asked about a top buggy. Cliffy said sure, he'd rig one out and fetch it up in a jiffy. He was still watching those Swallowtail men, but, when they angled in toward the curbing across the road, Cliffy relaxed. They were obviously in town early to get a load of supplies. He turned and went shuffling down toward the rental rigs at the back of the barn, leaving Given up at the doorway.

In fact, old Cliffy had no further thoughts about O'Brien or Given for perhaps ten or fifteen minutes, not until he heard a gunshot up front. By that time he had the horse buckled between the shafts anyway, so he dropped everything and went loping up toward the roadway. He had his .45 buckled around his middle, although he rarely ever wore the thing in town and later on couldn't account for the hunch that had made him put it on this morning. The first thing he saw was Bruce Horn, Sr., sagging against the front of Charley's store, holding both hands to his lower left side and looking all gray and shaky. Bruce, Sr., was the local blacksmith. It had been his big, overgrown son Given had prevented from giving that orphan kid a licking a few days earlier.

Given was down on one knee out front, to the right of where Cliffy skidded to a halt, perplexed and shocked at the sight of blood squeezing out through Bruce Horn's clenched fingers over across the way. Standing slightly behind the blacksmith and a little to one side of him was one of those Swallowtail cowboys that had come to town with Colin O'Brien on the wagon seat. He was staring straight over where Given was kneeling, and he had a cocked six-gun pushed into Bruce Horn's back. Without any of them uttering a word, it was very clear that, if Given fired his drawn gun, that cowboy over there was going to kill the blacksmith.

Cliffy stood like stone, unwilling to believe his own eyes. He didn't know that particular Swallowtail rider but that didn't mean anything. The country was full of cowboys he didn't know. They came and they went; they were a fiddle-footed breed of men. What held him stockstill was the dawning realization of what was going on over there. Charley Deems had the only steel safe in the whole countryside. It was a big black box that must've weighed two tons. It had a fine gold-painted eagle on its front and the maker's name, also in gold lettering, down at the bottom of the front door.

Charley had been accepting deposits from folks to stow in that big iron box for six or seven years now, and it had never once been assaulted. Local opinion, influenced no doubt by the formidable size and heft of that safe, held that nothing less than ten sticks of dynamite would even dent that door. This was very true, of course. What local opinion had *not* taken into consideration was that seasoned outlaws probably wouldn't ever try to blow that safe open, but would do exactly what was patently being done right now. They'd walk in some early morning, shove a cocked pistol under Charley's nose, and quietly order him to open the safe by its legal combination.

Cliffy's Adam's apple jerked. His shoulders stiffened. *Colin O'Brien!* Colin O'Brien was an *outlaw?* It was preposterous. It was incredible. It was . . . That man over there behind Bruce Horn said: "Put up the gun, Given, and stand up."

Cliffy's moving glance saw Given slowly obey. Slowly get back up to his feet and stand there, trading stares with the range rider.

"I ought to plug you just for meanness," the cowboy said, barely raising his voice. "You been actin' like the cock o' the walk ever since you hit Younger."

Given's reply was just as calm and quiet. "Go ahead. The minute you move that gun, I'll drop you like a ton of lead. Try it, if you doubt me."

Cliffy painfully swallowed again. He looked as far up the roadway as he could see. It was too early for many folks to be abroad yet. He looked southward, down toward Jim Crawford's jail house. There was nothing down there, either. At least he saw nothing, but then the side of the roadway obstructed his view. He was back in the gloom of the barn's musty runway. Evidently that outlaw over there behind Bruce Horn couldn't see Cliffy.

He moved a little to see if there'd been any reaction from across the road. There wasn't any. He began gently to slide to the right until he was entirely cut off from view outside. He stood a moment and let all his breath run out. He had $3,000 cash in that iron box of Charley's. It took a long time to save $3,000. He'd never had any very clear idea why he'd saved that money. He was a single man, too old to start any new ventures, and his day-to-day profit was more than enough for his simple needs. Still, it was *his* money. The idea of someone — especially someone like black-Irish Colin O'Brien whom he'd never cared for — taking it away from him in this fashion made old Cliffy mad clean through. He turned and hastened down the runway, out into the back alley, cut left, and ran along to the passageway between his building and the neighboring building, worked his way back up toward the roadway again, halted just far enough back so that he could spy the front of Charley's store without being seen himself.

A second cowboy came strolling southward from up by the Territorial Saloon, leading two horses. This man's head constantly swung from side to side. It stopped moving only when the man saw Bruce over there, reeling, with his bloody hands clasped to his ribs. The cowboy behind Bruce said something curtly to the man with the horses, and that man stopped before he got between Given and his friend. He turned and gave Given a quick, hard look. Obviously he'd been warned about getting between his partner and the man over in front of Cliffy's barn.

A moment later O'Brien walked forth from Charley's store. He had Deems with him. The merchant was as white as a sheet. His mouth was tugged down, giving him a look of extreme anguish. O'Brien stayed behind Charley and halted when his companions spoke. O'Brien looked, saw Given across the road, and for a second Cliffy could have sworn he saw the gun in O'Brien's hand move. But Colin reconsidered evidently, for he gave a curt order to his companions. They went around the horses in the roadway, leaving Bruce Horn to teeter back against the front of the store, grimacing, stepped over leather, and threw down on Edward Given who hadn't moved after putting up his six-gun and regaining his feet.

O'Brien then shoved Charley ahead, kept his gun on him until Charley was the only one of them still on the ground, then Colin kicked loose a stirrup, barked at

Deems, and Charley awkwardly and grudgingly swung up behind O'Brien's saddle.

Cliffy was sure the three of them would not break away in a wild run northward toward the mountains. They didn't, either; they turned and rode slowly southward down the full length of Younger's main thoroughfare. They even rode past Jim Crawford's jail house without so much as trotting.

Cliffy stepped forth onto the plank walk. On his right Edward Given, beginning at last to move, said, "Get out of the way," as he advanced down the plank walk. Cliffy didn't obey. Instead, he, too, started southward. It was clear that O'Brien, riding behind his two cohorts with Charley Deems protecting O'Brien's back, knew exactly what he was doing. It also seemed very probable that once the three outlaws were clear of town they'd either shoot Charley or bend a pistol barrel over his skull, dump him beside the road, and rake their horses into a belly-down run.

Cliffy was several doors north of the jail house when Given snarled at him from back a few feet. "Damn you, don't walk in front of me. Get off to one side! They're going to jettison that storekeeper now."

Cliffy swerved to one side, but he neither looked back at Given nor slackened his pace.

It was an unreal situation. Over in front of the barbershop someone broke into loud laughter and, farther back, eastward of the town's main business section, a shrill-voiced boy was calling a cow in to be milked. All around, the town was blandly going about its normal business. Cliffy and Given passed two old men strolling along, arguing about the snow pack in the mountains and whether or not this would be a drought summer. Neither old man paid the slightest attention to Cliffy or Edward Given.

What made it even more unreal was that gunshot which had been fired earlier. Ordinarily, in an orderly place like Younger, a gunshot brought folks boiling out like flies around a honey tree. Especially so early in the morning. This time, for some unknown reason, the gunshot had gone unnoticed. Cliffy and Edward Given seemed to be the only people in town who'd heard the shot or who'd witnessed that daring daylight robbery.

On ahead, O'Brien drew rein, peered around to Charley Deems, decided he didn't need his hostage any more, and raised his six-gun to club the merchant over the head. One of those onward outlaws also halted, but the foremost man kept right on riding. That halted cowboy was slightly ahead and to the right of O'Brien, in clear view.

Deems saw what his fate was soon to be, gave a squawk, and flung himself sideways. O'Brien's descending pistol barrel came down and didn't connect. He whipped around in the saddle and cried out — "Run for it!" — at the same time bending low and hooking his horse hard. The beast gave a tremendous bound, lit far ahead, and dug in with all four hoofs. O'Brien raced past his companion.

Given ripped out an oath as that cowboy left behind also raked his mount. The cowboy, seeing Given back there, and old Cliffy, threw out his right arm to fire at them. Cliffy drew and shot once, from the hip. The

77

cowboy dropped his gun, made no attempt at all to hang on, but slid down the left side of his frightened horse, and struck the ground like a sack of flour. He bounced and rolled and fetched up sprawled out, face down. He never moved again.

On ahead Colin O'Brien twisted, took in the scene behind him, and fired. His shots were disconcerting but wildly inaccurate. Neither Given nor old Cliffy even heard the lead strike anywhere close by. Given drew and fired twice, then swore heartily because O'Brien and the other robber were far beyond six-gun range. Cliffy did not fire again. He was standing there, looking at the man he'd killed.

From the jail house Jim Crawford's startled roar came forth one second ahead of the deputy himself. All that firing had taken place not more than fifty feet from his office. Jim had his pistol out. He was hatless and wild-eyed when he hit the plank walk. Given called to him, gesturing in the direction of the escaping men with his upraised pistol. Jim whirled and stared, but by then it was all over.

Charley Deems was on his feet now, soiled and rumpled from his tumble off Colin's animal. He was standing there, stupidly looking from the dead man close by up to where old Cliffy and Edward Given still stood. He seemed either unable to move or unwilling to.

Given put up his gun and joined Jim Crawford in hiking on down to where Cliffy's victim lay. For several moments longer Cliffy remained rooted, then he, too, walked on down.

Elsewhere, back up the roadway, men's shouts in quick alarm bounced back and forth off the store fronts. There was a quick pounding of booted feet and cries of warning. No one seemed to understand yet exactly what all that gunfire had been about. Someone was yelling for a doctor. Evidently Bruce Horn had been found in front of Charley's store with his bloody wound.

Cliffy halted where Jim Crawford had turned the dead man over. He gazed at the lifeless face, thought he'd seen this rider before, and fell to emptying his expended pistol casing and plugging in a fresh load from his belt.

Jim Crawford said: "Which one of you nailed him?"

Given jerked his head. Jim looked at old Cliffy working over his gun. "Right between the eyes," he murmured. "Cliffy, I'd never have believed it of you. You're a dead shot with that thing."

Cliffy said in a low mutter: "Never mind that. O'Brien made off with three thousand dollars of mine."

CHAPTER
FOUR

It took a lot of straightening out. For one thing, not until Given and Cliffy went up to the doctor's house to see Bruce Horn did anyone figure out why that first gunshot hadn't attracted attention. According to the blacksmith he'd been inside the store buying a box of Number Six city-head horseshoe nails when O'Brien and his friends walked in. O'Brien hadn't wasted a second. He'd thrown down on Charley and Bruce and ordered Charley to open the safe. Bruce had started to say something; he did not now remember exactly what it was. One of those Swallowtail cowboys had fired from a distance of no more than ten feet. The slug had ripped through Bruce's flesh below the ribs and had almost knocked him down. It wasn't a fatal injury, it wasn't even a serious one, in fact, but, as Bruce said, he hadn't known any of that at the time, and, because the wound was painful, he'd thought he'd been nearly killed.

The noise of that blast, Given suggested, had been directed outward across the roadway. He'd heard it very clearly and from instinct, thinking himself under attack, had dropped to one knee and had drawn his own weapon. He saw that cowboy herding wounded Bruce Horn outside, his intention clearly to employ the blacksmith as his shield and also as a hostage to guarantee the success of the robbery with Horn's life. It had worked, of course, and also this cleared up the minor mystery of that first gunshot.

Given and Jim Crawford went around to the general store. It was full of noisy people, mostly just curious but a few, like indignant old Cliffy Hart, shrilly demanding some kind of satisfaction about that money they'd lost.

For once Charley Deems was not the master of a situation in his establishment. He and Bill Haines from the Territorial Saloon were heatedly arguing when Crawford and Edward Given entered the store.

Rugged Bill was profanely saying that, if he'd thought for a moment Charley wouldn't have at least put up some token opposition to being robbed, he'd have kept his savings in his own strongbox, which was small enough to be carried away under a man's arm, but at least it wouldn't be carried away until Bill had been put down for good.

Charley's squeaky reply to this was logical, but Bill and the others were not right then susceptible to logic. "You think I was going to get killed for that money?" Charley squawked. "I tell you, Bill, Colin would have shot me in the back as easy as he'd have batted an eye. I've seen that look on men's faces before, an' I'm here to tell you . . ."

"Tell us nothing!" bawled old Cliffy. "Charley, you got to stand behind that safe. You got to make good our losses!"

Jim Crawford pushed through the crowd with Edward Given right behind him. Jim said to the angry people: "Leave him alone. We'll worry about gettin' the money back later. Right now I need some answers. Clear out, the lot of you. Go on, now. You too, Bill. Clear out."

The mob dispersed sullenly and reluctantly. Even old Cliffy walked out of the store, beside him scar-faced Bill Haines, chewing fiercely upon an unlighted cigar. Those two halted on the yonder plank walk and made some very pointed remarks about Charley's courage.

Deems was profusely perspiring. He mopped his face, looking exasperated. To Deputy Crawford he said: "What was I supposed to do . . . get killed? Colin'd have taken the money, anyway."

"Not if he didn't know the combination of the safe," stated Jim. "But forget that for now. Charley, what did he say to you when he pulled his gun?"

"Well, he said to open the safe."

"Anything else?"

"Of course, he said something else. He cocked that pistol and pushed it right up into my face, and, Jim, I tell you that barrel looked as big as a cannon. He said, 'Open up or I'll bust your skull like a pumpkin.' And he *meant* it."

"How about Bruce, what happened there?"

Deems looked a little less sure. "I'm not positive, but seems to me Bruce growled at one of them. The next thing I knew that cowboy had shot Bruce. That's when I went over and commenced opening the safe. Hell, Jim . . . what else can a man do in a position like that?"

"Nothing," said Edward Given placatingly. "Nothing at all, Mister Deems, unless he's hankerin' to be a dead hero, and that's no good because you can't hear the praise."

Charley looked at Given and his face smoothed out. "It's good to know there's one man in this damned town who understands," he muttered, relaxing enough to lean upon his counter. "Jim, whatever got into Colin?"

"You tell me how much money he got an' I'll tell you, Charley."

"Fourteen thousand dollars."

Crawford said nothing for a while; he simply stared at the storekeeper. Edward Given pursed his lips making a silent whistle. $14,000. That was more than most men made in a lifetime. It was a fortune.

Jim finally and dryly said: "That's your answer, Charley. But how did O'Brien know it was in there?"

Deems waggled his head disconsolately back and forth. "Dunno, Jim. Got no idea, unless because folks got to talking . . . like old Cliffy, for instance . . . he listened and put two and two together."

"Seven and seven," murmured Edward Given, but they paid no attention to him. He turned and strolled on over to gaze at the open safe, hands clasped behind his back, lips still pursed in that silent whistle.

There was nothing further to be learned from Charley Deems. Outside on the walk, Given asked Deputy Crawford about the Swallowtail cow outfit. Jim's answer was perfunctory; he was thinking about something else.

"It's owned by an Eastern syndicate. O'Brien's been the range boss out there for a number of years. I never liked the man personally, but he never gave us any real trouble here in town, either, so we sort of coasted along."

"He knew what he was doing this morning," murmured Given. "He knew exactly what he was doing."

Crawford turned to gaze at Given. He understood the other man's implication. "This country's full of folks I don't know a damned thing about, Mister Given, including you. But a feller can't go around asking personal questions. He'd either get shot or lied to."

Given let the implication go past that perhaps he might enlighten Jim about himself. He said, gazing across the road: "I have a buggy waiting for me over at Hart's barn, Deputy. Suppose you and I go for a little ride."

"If you mean after O'Brien, it might not be such a little ride."

They crossed over. Cliffy wasn't around but the rig was still back there, its beast in the shafts. They got in and drove up the runway, had reached the roadway exit, and were starting to turn southward when a big, thickly made gruff man atop a handsome chestnut sorrel gelding hailed Crawford.

"Banning," muttered Crawford. "Cuff Banning." He gestured Given to draw up.

Cuff Banning was a bold, aggressive, large man six feet tall and close to 200 pounds in weight. He was handsome in a weathered, rugged fashion. He was also forward and blunt in his gruff speech, as Given learned

84

the moment he halted the rig just outside Cliffy's barn and Banning drew in beside them to bend down and peer in at Crawford.

"Hell of a note," the cattleman boomed gruffly. "Hold-up right in plain sight. Colin O'Brien, too, of all people."

Jim said nothing. He seemed to understand the big man, to believe more was coming, and more was.

Banning straightened up, speared Edward Given with a look, and swore. "You're not goin' after them in *that?*" he asked, looking scornfully at the top buggy. "Jim, they'll head into the forest an' leave you high 'n' dry."

"Maybe," assented the deputy. "See you later, Cuff." He nudged Given, who drove on. As they were passing down through the excited town, Crawford drawled in his Arkansas twang: "Banning's a good man, only it takes a little getting used to . . . the way he fairly bellers at you when he talks. He's one of the biggest cowmen west of town. Runs something like seven thousand cows alone, they tell me."

"Did he have any money in Deems's safe?" asked Given, putting the town behind them and clucking the horse up into a rapid trot.

"No. The ranchers, if they got any money left over, don't fetch it to town." Crawford adjusted to the jostling of the buggy, was silent for a time, then musingly said: "Fourteen thousand dollars. I don't understand there bein' that much. Usually Charley doesn't have more'n maybe six, seven thousand in his steel box."

Given handed the lines to Crawford, reached inside his shirt pocket, brought forth a tobacco sack, and bent to making a cigarette. After he'd lighted up, he pushed back his hat and leaned there, smoking, with both elbows on his knees. He was intently watching the onward roadway.

Jim went on puzzling things out aloud while he drove, his lantern-jawed face drawn up into a painful grimace. "Right now folks are blamin' Charley, but by tomorrow they'll also be haulin' me over the coals. Damned if I had any inkling there was a stick-up goin' on until you and old Cliffy opened up outside my window. At least, it sure sounded like you were shootin' outside the window. And Cliffy droppin' that one the way he did, I'll be damned if I ever had any idea he could shoot like that."

Given said disinterestedly: "Any man wearing a gun ought to be able to shoot, or he shouldn't wear a gun."

Jim turned his head. "Like you, Mister Given?"

Given didn't answer that. He drew up sharply and pointed ahead, saying: "Cut off the road here, Deputy. Turned right up through the trees. Here's where they left the road."

Crawford hauled the horse around. He began hanging out the side to watch for fresh tracks, too. Neither of them had anything to say for a full mile. Given was too engrossed in horse tracks and Jim, also watching the tracks, had additionally to guide the horse through the trees. All he said that first mile was: "Good thing they turned west instead of east. From here on the forest's pretty thin, but over east of the road them danged trees are thicker'n flies in August."

What eventually stopped them weren't trees; it was a sheer-banked little dry wash that ran straight across their onward route. Given got down, went ahead, and studied the land while Crawford tethered the horse. When they came together at the edge of the wash, Given was standing with his head bowed, his cigarette dead between his lips.

Jim stepped around and pointed. "Yonder they go . . . southward now." Given nodded but kept on staring at the ground. Crawford turned. "Are you comin'?"

Given removed his smoke, saw that it was too short to be re-lighted, and tossed it down into the dry wash that was about ten feet deep and sandy along its base. He started along and Jim went on his way tracking those two riders to where there was a buck run that led down into the wash, up the opposite side, and disappeared westward through the trees.

"Wait a minute," sang out Given, as Crawford started to cross over. "Why west, Deputy?"

Jim stepped back onto firm ground and rolled his brows together. "Why west? What d'you mean . . . why west?"

Given rocked his head to one side, indicating the southward flow of countryside. "Open country down there, Deputy, as near as I can make out. If I was running from the law, damned if I'd head west . . . unless I had a very good reason . . . when the lay of southward land was so much better."

Jim pondered this and came up with nothing. "O'Brien knows the country westerly like he knows the inside of his hand."

"Doesn't he know the southward range, too, Deputy?"

"Well, yes, he does. But I'd say, knowing the things about Colin O'Brien that've come out since this morning, that he'd have every camp site from here to wherever he's going fixed in his mind damned well in advance."

Given accepted this with a slight nod while he skeptically studied Crawford. "The last week or so I've driven around the country a little, too, and southward from Younger there's nothing but flat land for more miles than a man could cover in several days. No buildings, no cow camps that I saw, no chance of running into riders."

"That's right enough, Mister Given. But if he's heading west, it's because he's got a —"

"Deputy. Westward there are ranches and riders and cow camps." Given squinted at the sun to estimate the time of day. When he lowered his face, Jim was watching him suspiciously.

"What're you gettin' at, Mister Given?"

"That O'Brien knows exactly where he's going, as you said, and it's not too far west. Maybe just far enough to leave a lot of tracks. Tell me something, Deputy. Is there a rocky place west of here where horse tracks wouldn't show?"

"Sure. More than one."

"And southward . . . is there any such place southward?"

Jim reached up to tilt back his hat. He was beginning to follow Given's train of thought. He shook his head and was silent for a moment. Given turned and started strolling back the way they had come. He, too, was silent.

Through the eastward trees they heard a band of hard-riding men approaching. Given was untying the buggy horse and stopped to look and listen. "Deputy," he said, "I'll make you a bet. I'll give you odds this'll be your big, blustery friend, Banning."

It was. Banning came out of the forest, saw the rig, and hauled back on the reins. Jim looked from Cuff to the men with him. They were mostly cowboys from the outlying ranches with a scattering of townsmen, including old Cliffy Hart. Banning boomed out a question as his horse skidded to a jamming halt.

"Which way do the tracks go?"

Jim pointed southward along the edge of the dry wash. Without another word Banning turned and tore away, gesturing for his companions to come along. The dust was thick for several moments as that posse plunged away. As it began to settle, Given turned the buggy, climbed up, and curbed the fore wheel so Crawford could also climb in. Given then began a leisurely drive back toward town.

"What're you figurin'?" Jim asked when they were back on the stage road.

"That there's a sight more here than meets the eye, Deputy. A good deal more."

"Such as?"

"Why go west and risk discovery, why head back into country where he'd be recognized? Why make for some rock ledge where Banning and his posse are going to lose the tracks . . . unless O'Brien's got something in mind besides just robbing Deems's safe?"

"All right," Crawford said, leaning back. "You've got the right questions, Mister Given. Suppose you also give me some right answers."

"Can't yet."

"But you're thinkin' O'Brien's goin' to hit the town again."

"Not necessarily. The other day, when I met him in the roadway, O'Brien didn't strike me as a fool."

"He isn't. He's ornery and opinionated . . . and a lousy outlaw, too, it seems . . . but he's not dumb."

"Then whatever his reason is, Deputy, it's got to be a very good one. Anyway, my guess is that he's not hell-bent out of the country at all. He wants folks to believe that, of course, but you judge men by their actions, and O'Brien's actions are either the actions of a fool . . . or of a man with something more than just robbing Deems's safe on his mind. He's going to show up in Younger again. I'll bet you a good horse and saddle on that."

Crawford scowled but he didn't argue. He did, though, just before they got back to town, begin covertly studying Edward Given because, gunfighter or not, Given was obviously no fool, either.

CHAPTER
FIVE

The morning stage left a letter for Jim Crawford over at Charley Deems's store the day after the robbery. Jim didn't pick up that letter until noon when he was on his way down to the café after questioning everyone he could think of who might have even a suspicion of where O'Brien and his sidekick might go, if they didn't leave the country.

No one had any very sensible suggestions, though, and Cuff Banning, back in town again after his abortive chase, confirmed something Given had said. He and his men had lost the outlaws' trail four miles west where an obsidian sink had to be crossed. Banning said they'd searched on the other side of the sink for tracks, but hadn't found them. It was Banning's idea that O'Brien had holed up somewhere near that sink until nightfall, then had gone southward out of the country. Banning also told Crawford he'd sent two of his best riders scouting down through the lower ranges for some sight or news of the outlaws.

Crawford had his dinner and sauntered over to the jail house to read the letter from his boss, the county sheriff. He had a letter to write, too, but he wasn't at all enthusiastic about it; reporting the robbery to the sheriff wasn't going to be easy.

Given was sitting in the office when Crawford walked in. Jim was too surprised to take the letter from his pocket until after he'd crossed to the desk, but then he didn't open it because it was obviously the reply to Jim's earlier letter to the county seat seeking information concerning one Edward Given.

"I think I've got this thing doped out," stated Given, without any preliminaries. "I thought about it most of the night. The rest of the night I patrolled the town."

Jim's eyebrows dropped. "You what? Patrolled the town? What for?"

"O'Brien," stated Given succinctly. "Whatever it is he's after is here. I'm convinced of that."

"Or out at the Swallowtail," Crawford grunted. "He spent a sight more time out there than he spent in town."

Given did not pursue that tangent. All he said about it was that he'd sent Rusty Miller, the orphan kid he'd befriended, out to lie low and watch all the people who came and went at the Swallowtail headquarters ranch.

Jim was scandalized. "That kid could get killed, Given, confound it. You had no right to do that. Besides, if you've got anything worthwhile, then it's your chore to turn it over to the law."

"I don't have anything the law would be particularly interested in, Deputy. At least, not yet. Besides, I warned the boy. He's smart and he's careful. Being an orphan teaches you early in life to look close before you move."

"How would you know?"

"Because I was an orphan, Deputy," stated Given, giving Crawford a long look. "That's what you were fishing for, wasn't it, something about my past?"

Jim faintly reddened and removed his hat. "Folks're saying around town that I'm not doing all I should in this thing."

Given nodded. "You expected that, didn't you? Hell, no peace officer ever does all he should do. If you doubt me, ask the taxpayers. Forget that for now and tell me something. How long has Charley Deems been here in Younger?"

"Charley?" Crawford exclaimed dumbly. "Why, I'd say he's been around six, seven years. Why?"

"What do you know about him?"

"Nothing much. He came here with a little money and a trader's wagon, set up shop, and he's been here ever since. He prospered right from the start. We had a general store before he came, but it was run by an old cuss who was hard of hearing and who had the complaint so bad he was only open about two, three days out of the week."

"Was this other storekeeper in the same building where Charley now is?"

"Yeah. In fact, Charley bought out what little stock he had along with the building. What about it?"

Given gazed out the open doorway. It was one of those ice clear, warm, early summer days with pine fragrance in the air and the sounds of activity around. Normally, perhaps, a man would wish to go out into the shade and doze or maybe have a smoke, and just sop up the benevolence of nature in the high desert country.

Not Edward Given. He said: "I'll tell you what I think, Deputy. I think it wasn't any accidental discovery of O'Brien's that let him know there was fourteen thousand dollars in that safe. I think someone told him. I think that same someone is also the reason he's still in the country. There's something else planned."

Jim said in a low whisper: "Charley? Are you sayin' Charley told Colin there was all that money in his safe?"

Given brought his gaze back from the golden roadway. "Deputy, I've spent the day and part of last night asking questions. All I've gotten so far was the same reaction you showed yesterday when you learned how much money was in the safe. Surprise. Haines up at the saloon even told me he didn't believe there'd ever before been that much in cash in Younger."

"He ought to know," agreed Crawford. "But about Charley . . . ?"

"Deputy, I'm trying to explain this to you. No one else had any inkling so much was here. Except Charley Deems. Some men I've known would wait even longer than seven years to get hold of that much cash all in one place. That's why I'm curious about Charley's past."

Jim stroked his scratchy jaw. He hadn't shaved since the day before. The sound of his stroking hand was like tiny grains of sand being ground over glass. "I can find out," he finally muttered, "but it'll take time. There won't be another stage through for a few days. Then I'll send a letter to the sheriff over at the county seat. He can dig up all we need by using the telegraph."

"Take too long," stated Given, and stood up. "I've got to be at the boarding house when the boy returns. I told him to get back before sundown."

Crawford sat on after Given had departed, turning the thought over and over in his mind about Charley Deems. He had no affection for Charley. He didn't actually dislike him. It was just Charley's manner of looking down his nose at everyone.

He tried to recall whether he'd seen Colin O'Brien and Charley together. There were times when he'd seen them standing together up at Bill Haines's place. But there was nothing to that, either. At least, up until now, there hadn't been. O'Brien knew Charley Deems the same as everyone else who traded at the general store knew him. But as for tying those two together, Jim couldn't do it.

Remembering the letter, he drew it forth from his pocket, slit the envelope, smoothed out the inside paper upon the desk, and set forth to decipher laboriously the sheriff's cramped handwriting. The more he read, the longer his face got.

The sheriff knew Edward Given. It seemed that Given had been a Wells Fargo express detective for the past ten years. Before that he'd been a deputy U.S. marshal over in Kansas. Prior to that he'd been a county sheriff down in New Mexico Territory. The sheriff also wrote that, if Ed Given was in his area, he wished Crawford would ask him to come to the county seat because there was an opening at one of the towns up by Whitman and the sheriff would like nothing better than to have a man of Given's character and experience take the job.

Crawford sighed, folded the letter, popped it back into his pocket, and scooped up his hat. No wonder Given seemed so experienced at something like the Deems affair. Jim had been mighty curious about that the day before when the two of them had been returning to town. Given second-guessed Colin O'Brien right down the line. No novice could have done that. In fact, Cuff Banning, whose range adjoined Swallowtail's range and who'd known O'Brien a number of years, hadn't been able to do that.

Crawford went along to Agatha Beeman's rooming house but Given wasn't there. He strolled back to Cliffy's barn but Given wasn't there, either. He disengaged himself from old Cliffy's acrimonious garrulousness and hiked over to the Territorial Saloon. There, he found his man. Given and Bill Haines were having a drink, each of them drawing from their private stock.

Bill grunted a dour greeting and reached under the bar for another glass. He regarded Crawford dourly. Given, on the other hand, was affable, although he didn't smile. In fact, Crawford had never seen him smile.

While he watched Bill pour his drink, Jim fished out that letter from the county seat and tossed it down before Given. He reared back his head, downed the liquor, and set his glass in front of Bill.

Haines corrugated his brows. "You think whiskey'll make you lose some of the lead in your britches, Jim, so's maybe you can take after O'Brien before next winter?"

"Just pour!" exclaimed the deputy. "Just pour." From the edge of his eye he watched Given read that letter, refold it without showing anything upon his face, and push it back over next to Jim's refilled glass.

Given said: "Tell him I'm not interested in that job, Deputy." Given flagged for Haines to refill his glass, also. He leaned with both elbows atop the bar and gazed at his own likeness in the back-bar mirror. "When a man's given nearly two-thirds of his best years to a profession," he said very quietly, "that ought to be enough."

Crawford didn't touch his second drink. He said: "All right, Marshal, but why all the secrecy? Most fellers'd be right proud to have your background."

"No secrecy, Deputy. At least no deliberate secrecy. I came here because I heard Younger was the drowsiest town in Oregon, with no telegraph, no newspaper, and only one stage through a week. I want to get a piece of land and build a cabin, have a few horses, and spend my time fishing and maybe doing a little hunting."

Bill Haines looked sympathetic, then he scowled again and said: "Younger *used* to be a drowsy place . . . except for Saturday nights. Not any more. And say, Mister Given, did Jim just call you 'Marshal'?"

Given lifted his drink without replying, so Crawford unfolded the letter, spun it around, and also sipped his whiskey. When Haines finished reading, he looked from beneath his shaggy brows at Given.

Given looked right back.

Crawford got an odd feeling in the pit of his stomach. The look those two exchanged was wary and careful, and not especially friendly. He cleared his throat.

"Did the kid get back yet?" he asked Given.

"He got back. I gave him a dollar an' told him to go buy a big steak for supper."

Haines gently refolded the letter and pushed it away from him back toward Jim Crawford. He then poured himself a double jolt and drank it straight down. Jim watched this; he'd never seen Bill do that before. As a matter of fact, Bill Haines seldom drank at all.

Given turned and gazed upward. His face was expressionless. "Care to take a little ride tonight, Deputy?" he asked.

"I reckon so. Where to?"

"Meet me at the livery barn at sundown and find out." Given turned back to regarding Bill Haines. "How about you, Haines, care for a little exercise tonight?"

Bill stared and slowly nodded. Once again, Crawford got that peculiar twinge behind his belt buckle. There was something going on here between those two older men. Also, once again, he broke it up with words.

"Something the kid told you, Mister Given, that you want to look into?"

"Yeah."

"Like maybe he saw O'Brien out at Swallowtail?"

Given straightened up off the bar. "Meet me at the livery barn at sundown and find out," he replied, turned on his heel, and walked out of the place.

Crawford got to pondering. As Bill Haines started to move off, he said: "Bill, you two fellers have an argument or something before I walked in?"

"No," the barman growled, reaching for the three empty glasses.

"That was quite a look you give him after readin' the sheriff's letter, Bill."

Haines flared up. "Mind your own consarned business. Instead of pryin' where you got no business, go out an' find Colin an' my money, damn it all!"

Jim watched Haines's red, angry face a moment, then also turned and strolled out of the saloon. Sometimes a man just couldn't make heads or tails out of things. There were days like that.

CHAPTER
SIX

When Haines showed up at the livery barn, he was grumpy. He and Given were sniping back and forth when Jim Crawford arrived. Bill was complaining he'd had to hire an extra night bartender — which was five bucks shot to hell — and on top of that he must've been out of his mind when he'd agreed to take this ride.

Ed Given's reply was brisk and pointed. "You can't see beyond the end of your nose, Haines, and you never could. Go on back and save that five dollars. On a ride like this I'm not sure I could stomach you, anyway."

Bill might have pursued that remark but for Jim. Crawford growled at the two of them, then stepped around into the barn, and craned around for Cliffy. He wasn't there. Jim stepped back outside again. Given pointed. At the tie rack stood three saddled animals. One of them belonged to Jim. "Don't like to waste time," Given said. "Let's go."

They got astride and followed the ex-lawman out of town. The sun had set, but dusk had not yet arrived. There was an iron-like dull shading to the sky which accompanied that stillness which usually arrived at day's ending.

"What'n hell did you strap this saddle boot and Winchester to my saddle for?" Bill Haines demanded, when they were well away from Younger. "You figure to go wolf huntin' in the dark, Given?"

Crawford was a little puzzled. Haines wasn't an exuberantly genial man ever, but neither had he ever shown himself as pointedly sour as he'd been doing since their earlier meeting at the saloon. Jim growled: "What's got into you, Bill? You're actin' like a spoiled kid. A saddle gun can be handy in lots of ways. But that isn't it, is it?"

"I told you before," piped Haines. "Mind your own consarned business!"

"I'm makin' this my business," snapped Crawford, stung a little. "What the hell's wrong with you, anyway?"

Haines didn't answer. He didn't look in Jim's direction again, either, for another long mile. He glowered at Given's back or he swung his head around to watch the countryside. But at least he kept silent.

Given seemed to know exactly where he was going, which inclined Crawford to believe the former lawman had scouted this country before. He stopped in a belt of pines once and built a smoke. All he said about this delay was that it wasn't getting dark as rapidly as he'd thought it would. They were then less than a mile from the Swallowtail home ranch, which Jim had long since deduced was their objective.

Bill Haines still had that unfriendly look on his face, but when Given glanced at him, offering his tobacco sack, Bill took it and also worked up a cigarette. As he handed the makings back, he looked Given straight in the eye.

"You playin' cat and mouse?" he asked quietly, and, when the ex-lawman shook his head, Bill said: "Then what's in your mind, Given?"

"Needed a man I could trust," stated Given enigmatically, turned, and rode on.

None of this little exchange was meant to convey anything to Crawford, but Jim hadn't arrived on earth in the last rain. He began to have an inkling about what lay between these two graying men. But he said nothing and showed nothing.

They broke clear of the last pines where several hundred acres of land had been cleared long before. There were a few burned-out stumps here and there, but mostly the land was totally devoid of any sign that the forest had ever existed at all in this area. It was turning gloomy now.

Given pointed. "Are those the lights from Swallowtail?" he asked. Both Crawford and Bill said they were. Jim, more familiar with the big ranch, added something more to his assent.

"See that pair of small orange squares off to the right? That's the bunkhouse where the riders stay. The larger light over to our left is from the main house."

"Who lives at the main house, Deputy?"

"Well. Colin O'Brien used to, Mister Given. I don't know who'll be over there now."

"But someone obviously *is* over there, Deputy . . . otherwise there'd be no lights. Doesn't that seem natural to you?"

Crawford didn't get to answer. Bill Haines said: "Given, quit playin' games. You know damned well who

102

you figure's in the main house. If we're goin' on up there, let's get to riding."

Given turned and studied Bill a moment. "That's something I've always liked about you," he said. "You make a decision, Bill, and you move. No shilly-shallying around."

Haines squirmed in his saddle but said nothing. He didn't even look at the ex-marshal. But Given was in command here and he didn't move out. He dismounted and motioned for his companions to do the same. He yanked out his carbine, tied his horse to a low limb, and waited with his back to the forest for the others to finish and walk on over. When they did, he spat out his dead smoke, told the other two men to make certain their carbines were loaded, and then he started out across the clearing.

Crawford, taking the long measure of all that onward open range, hissed at Given: "If anything happens over there, we're goin' to be one hell of a long way from the horses."

Haines had the answer to that. "Yeah, but if they're watchin', Jim, they'll skyline us ridin' in a quarter mile before we even get close. His way's the best . . . much as I hate to admit it."

Given kept right on walking. The others hastened to catch up, then the three of them moved along for a considerable distance. When Given halted eventually, Haines said softly: "All right, what'd the kid see out here?"

"O'Brien," replied Given, turning his head from side to side.

"I thought so," mumbled Haines, and also began testing the night. "They'll have a sentry out, Given. You can bet on that."

Jim's feeling that these two were old hands at this business prompted him to ask dryly in that Arkansas drawl of his: "Tell me something. When you boys did this before, were you on the same side?"

Both Haines and Given turned to stare coldly a moment before they went forward once more without a word being said between them. Crawford smiled to himself in the dark. Obviously Given and Haines had *not* been on the same side before, and, since Given had spent all his previous years as a lawman, it took no great deductive power to guess that Bill had been outside the law. Crawford walked along, still pleased with himself. Not that he particularly cared what Bill had been somewhere else; he couldn't be responsible for what had happened somewhere else years earlier. Still, it was interesting to know these things.

Haines hissed and dropped to one knee when they were close enough to the ranch buildings to scent wood smoke and cooking. He pointed dead ahead where the yard began. Beyond that pale place stood the huge log barn, the dimly discernible bunkhouse, and off to their left, the low, rambling main ranch house. Closer, though, where a tiny scarlet glow faintly showed, sometimes brightening, sometimes fading, pale starlight wetly reflected off dark steel.

"He's a damned fool," Haines whispered, "smokin' like that. You can spot a cigarette tip glowin' and fadin'

104

like that for a mile. If I had an Injun's bow and a couple of arrers, I could salt him down without a sound."

Given kept watching that sentry for a long time. He turned his head and made a slow, very careful study of the other points around the yard where another sentry might be also waiting, but there was no other sign of one. Jim, too, strained ahead to make certain there was only this one watcher. Jim was beginning to get restless. Given and Haines squatted there like a pair of stone idols, acting as though time had stopped. They didn't even move their heads. Finally Haines leaned inward and whispered to Given.

"One to the left, one to the right. We can find him if we're careful . . . and quiet."

Given offered no response for a long time. So long, in fact, Crawford didn't think he was going to pass on Bill's suggestion. But ultimately he turned. It seemed to Jim as though these two older men weren't even conscious of his presence. They were acting out some system of attack they alone seemed fully to comprehend.

"Finding him's not the point exactly, Bill," murmured Given. "We know he's there and I think I know *why* he's there. But the first move we make to get him, all hell's going to bust loose."

"Then what'll we do?" queried Haines.

"We go back."

Haines was no less startled than Jim Crawford was. He hissed at Given. "*What*? What the hell's wrong with you, Ed? We come out to find him, didn't we?"

"Yes. And we've done that. Come on." Given got up, turned, and started back toward the horses. Crawford stared after him. So did Bill Haines, and it was Bill who got up stiffly and went along behind Given first, snarling to himself under his breath.

Crawford caught up with Given and halted him. He looked down at the shorter man suspiciously. "You afraid three guns can't take him, Marshal? Let me tell you something. Those Swallowtail men over there'll back off the second they know it's the law."

Given looked annoyed but he controlled himself long enough to say thinly: "Let me tell *you* something, Deputy. You think you know those cowboys and maybe you do . . . when they're ridin' for wages . . . but that's changed now, otherwise O'Brien wouldn't be down there and that armed sentry wouldn't be makin' sure he wasn't interrupted. O'Brien's got fourteen thousand dollars, Deputy. That's twice as much as he needs to buy every rider Swallowtail has. And remember something else. O'Brien hired those men. He knew exactly what he was doing. We wouldn't stand a chance . . . not with O'Brien offerin' three or four hundred apiece to those men of his, and that's one reason why he had the guts to return. So's he'd be able to hire his own gang . . . and pay them in advance in cash! Now stop talking and *walk!*"

Given strode off. Crawford hung back a moment, putting it all together in his head. Bill Haines reached over, touched Jim's arm, and jerked his head. "He's right. Given's right. He doesn't make many mistakes, Jim, so come along."

Crawford went, but he stumped along with his head low in thought, for what had started out as a simple hold-up and robbery had abruptly become something much more complicated and confusing. When they reached the horses and were untying, Crawford asked Given what he thought all this was leading up to. Given didn't answer that until he was back across leather and leading the way eastward. Then he made another cigarette, handed Haines the sack, lit up, and mightily exhaled as he gazed skyward.

"Is there any more big money around?" he asked, and, when Jim shrugged and wagged his head negatively, Given gazed at him and said: "Then it's something else which could be just as profitable. What do you expect that'd be, Deputy?"

Haines was lighting his cigarette and spoke through pursed lips as he shook out his match. "Cattle. Swallowtail cattle. Maybe Swallowtail horses, too."

Given threw Bill a look that Crawford thought was sardonic, but Jim didn't spend much time on that. He closed his mind down around what Bill had said. It made sense, bitter sense, but nevertheless it made sense. Colin knew every inch of the countryside. He'd been ramrodding the Swallowtail roundups and drives ever since he'd been range boss. Jim groaned, "Oh, Lord," and slouched along, full of frightening thoughts. When they came back within sight of town again, he raised his head to say: "How big a fool does O'Brien take me for, comin' back like that?"

"Not for a fool at all, Deputy," explained Given. "He gives you credit for being smart enough to get up a posse and go hell-for-leather after him. He figured you were a dedicated lawman who'd fan out in every direction, looking for him, which is exactly what a good lawman would do. He also figured the last place you'd think to look for him would be his home place. His men think the same way, too, otherwise that sentry back there wouldn't have been careless enough to stand watch with a cigarette in his mouth."

Crawford couldn't quite swallow Given's logic in this. He thought the ex-lawman was trying to make him feel less a fool. But he didn't say anything, probably wouldn't have said anything anyway, but Bill spoke out, negating even the possibility, and Bill also made sense.

"Jim, you know more about Swallowtail than I do. Don't they usually make up their big drive this time of year . . . late spring . . . and head down toward the railroad at Carter Meadows?"

"Or north toward Salem," said Crawford. "One or the other. But, yeah, this is the time of year all the big outfits make their drives."

Given gave Haines another of those sardonic glances when he said: "Old dogs never forget, do they?" Before Bill could answer that, Given also said: "Deputy, you stay in Younger. O'Brien's foxy. He'll have someone watching you. I have an idea who that'll be, but anyway you stay in town, or, if you have to ride out, always go east or maybe northward . . . never southward or westward. We want O'Brien to think you're confounded. My kid and I'll do the spying on Swallowtail. You understand?"

Jim understood, but it rankled, so he said: "Marshal, you're goin' to get that kid killed, foolin' around with men like these." He squinted at the nearing town lights. "Besides, I can get all the help I need from the county seat."

"Sure," growled Bill Haines. "You fetch in a big posse and I can kiss my money goodbye. O'Brien'll leave the cattle and skip out of the country. Jim, you do like Given says." Bill cleared his throat and spat. He afterward concentrated hard on trimming all the ash off his cigarette. "Take my word for it, Given doesn't make many mistakes."

All the way back into town Haines rode along, looking at neither of his companions. His face was grim and tough-set. He would say no more.

They got to Cliffy's barn and ran head on into the old man himself. At sight of Haines, riding with Deputy Crawford and Edward Given, Cliffy looked astonished, and that gave them all an excellent opportunity to escape before he started in on Crawford about his vanished $3,000 again. It was by then well after midnight, and, except for Bill's bar and one or two other night spots, Younger was decently abed.

CHAPTER
SEVEN

Given sent Rusty Miller through the westward forest the following day and the day after that with specific instructions not to be seen. As he explained to Jim Crawford at the bar of Bill Haines's Territorial Saloon, a fifteen-year-old boy was just naturally elusive. They made a game of something like that the same as Indians also did, and, if they'd been knocked from pillar to post as young Rusty had, they'd be even harder to spot.

But the lad returned each evening with nothing to report.

Given got quietly thoughtful after that, and the third day, when folks were beginning to grumble openly that Jim wasn't doing anything to get back their money, Given wasn't even in town.

The following day, though, he was. Jim encountered him at the local café. Given and the orphan kid were having steaks for supper. The lad was small for his age, had a sprinkling of freckles across the saddle of a turned-up nose, and his clear blue eyes watched every move Given made with a look of admiration that made Jim remember his own boyhood and how he'd looked at his own father.

He asked Given if there was room at the table for one more. There was, and Jim flagged to the cook for the same supper steak, then he fixed Given with an intent gaze and said: "Missed seein' you in town yesterday."

Given went right on eating. He obviously was very hungry. Just as obviously he didn't mean for this relaxing time to be taken up by shop talk. He told the waiter, when he brought Jim's dinner, to fetch back two more tall glasses of milk, one for himself, one for Rusty.

Jim had coffee. He drank it a little at a time, waiting in vain for Given to speak. Given never did, except to the lad. Crawford might have been 100 miles away. Even the boy noticed this and seemed a little embarrassed by it. When Rusty slowed down, Given said he should finish everything on his plate to get meat under his ribs. But Rusty put aside his fork and Given didn't insist. When the meal was over, Given brought forth two cigars from an inside coat pocket, wordlessly handed one to Jim, and lit the other one himself. That was the first indication he'd given since Jim had seated himself at the table that he was aware of the deputy.

"Had enough?" he asked the orphan. When Rusty nodded, Given said: "How about goin' over and seein' if Cliffy grained the horse and put down fresh bedding?" Rusty jumped up, smiling. Given watched him cross out of the room with his eyes squeezed nearly closed, with cigar smoke trailing languidly up past his shrewd eyes, then he sighed and leaned back in the chair.

"Deputy, you know what it's like not to belong to anyone when you're his age?"

"No, can't say as I do, Mister Given. My pa was a fine man. So I had someone to belong to. Rusty's a good kid. From time to time I've watched him."

"So he's told me."

Jim looked up quickly, unable from the inflectionless way in which it had been said to read anything into it. Given nodded, removed his cigar, and carefully put it upon the edge of his empty plate.

"Well, that's not what you're here for, of course. But all the same that boy and I've got the same strong hankering, Deputy, a home and someone around who cares. I think we'll work it out between us."

"He'll be a lucky kid, Marshal. I couldn't wish anything better for him."

Given looked up to see if that was irony, saw that it wasn't, and cleared his throat. "O'Brien's making his gather," he said curtly. "Rusty didn't see it because O'Brien's no fool. I thought he had to be at it. That's where I was all day yesterday . . . southward about six miles."

"Southward?" Jim murmured, leaning forward a little. "But Swallowtail always make their gather up north where they've got separating corrals."

"Not this time, Deputy. I saw O'Brien."

"You *saw* him . . . are you plumb sure?"

Given took up the cigar and puffed a moment, then laid it aside again. "I'm plumb sure. I'd remember his face."

"How'd you get that close without being seen yourself?"

112

"Field glasses, Deputy. If he's gathering to the south, that means a drive down to rail's end at this place Haines called Carter Meadows. Is that right?"

"That's right."

"Well. From here on we're going to have to rely on your knowledge of that southward country. I'm not familiar with it except in a very general way."

"You figure we ought to let them start their drive?"

"I think so, Deputy," said Given, fishing for some change and putting it atop the table. "I'll meet you up at Bill's saloon in a half hour. The three of us'll talk a little."

"You figure to include Haines in this?"

Given stood up, nodding. "Yes. Haines is a good man in something like this. A *damned* good man."

"You two've known each other somewhere else, haven't you?"

Given turned away saying: "Ask *him*, Deputy. Ask Bill Haines. That's his story, not mine."

After Given's departure, Jim finished his meal and called for a second cup of coffee. He sat there deeply in thought, turning things over and over in his mind. He knew one thing — Swallowtail employed seven riders excluding the range boss, and not one of those men had ever impressed Jim Crawford as being timid or inexperienced. He used to believe Colin O'Brien hired men who seemed unnecessarily rough. Now he could understand the reason for that without any difficulty.

He was jarred out of his reverie when gruff Cuff Banning stamped over and dropped down at Given's empty place, tossed down his hat, and let off a big, ragged sigh.

"What a week this has been," Banning growled. "First that damned robbery, then, when we started our gather, we found the lousy cattle scattered from hell to breakfast."

Jim put down his empty cup and leaned back to work on that cigar Given had presented to him. He saw Banning eyeing him skeptically and puffed in silence, awaiting what he thought he knew the cowman would say next. He wasn't disappointed, either. Banning gave his order to the waiter, then hunched forward on the table.

"Jim, what's got into you? Folks're growlin' all over town about the way you let Colin get clean away with all that money. I never seen you act like this before. A feller can defend a friend just so far."

Jim smiled enigmatically. "I've been learnin' something about my own trade this past week, Cuff. I've been learning that when a man beats his backsides black and blue poundin' leather all over the countryside, he's using the wrong end of his anatomy to make a living with."

"Yeah? What's all that mean, Jim?"

"It means I'm using my head now. And as far as O'Brien's concerned . . . he's not lost yet. Not by a damned sight."

After saying that much, Crawford paid his tab and strolled out into the star-filled, warm evening, leaving big Cuff Banning sitting back there hunched over the table, gazing speculatively after him.

Cliffy Hart came along making snuffling sounds. He didn't see Jim Crawford until he was almost past, then he did, and he stopped to turn and darkly scowl. "What you doin', standin' around here suckin' on a stogie just like you didn't let my three thousand dollars get away? Jim Crawford, don't you know losin' all that money's goin' to put a crimp into this town folks'll be years gettin' over? It's not just my money I'm thinking about, either. It's all —"

"Shut up, will you, Cliffy."

The old liveryman's contorted face froze. His pale old eyes popped wide open. "Shut up," he whispered. "Shut up? Why you overgrown hop-toad, you!" Cliffy's voice was gaining power again, turning shrill and angry. He skipped up and down in violent indignation. "*You* tellin' *me* to shut up? Damn your lily-livered innards, Jim Crawford. I got a notion to punch you right in the . . ."

"Cliffy, Cliffy, quiet down. You're goin' to get your money back. But not if you act this way."

"My money back? Jim, what're you saying? Jim Crawford, consarn you anyway, are you keepin' back secrets? By golly, I never heard tell of a deputy actin' so . . . so . . ."

Jim let a tangy streamer of cigar smoke drift upward. He smiled at old Cliffy, turned, and paced on up toward the saloon. He couldn't recall ever feeling so confident about the solution of a crime before. He didn't know exactly why he felt that way. But he did, and, since he was not a complicated man, he paced along, smiling and smoking until a jarring thought

115

struck him. What if something should happen to Edward Given? For a fact, with O'Brien and seven hard-bitten range men gunning for anyone who might try to interfere with their secret scheme, Given just might stop a bullet.

Jim halted outside the Territorial, stepped to the edge of the walk, and threw away his cigar. When he squared back around, he wasn't smiling at all; in fact, he looked grim and unrelenting.

If Colin O'Brien or anyone like him tried to pot-shoot Edward Given, there was going to be a lot of lead flying, and that, Jim promised himself bleakly, was a damned fact!

He stepped inside and blinked against the quick, hard lash of lamplight. Haines's barroom was full of men. It was still early and fresh townsmen and riders kept entering the place. They were lined solidly along the bar from one end to the other. That red-headed, big, buxom girl Cuff Banning was sweet on was at a table with another girl, sharing a drink. At other tables men were gambling or just seriously drinking. For a while, because of the constant movement, the smoke, and dull monotone of deep voices, Crawford didn't spy Edward Given. But eventually he spotted him, over near the southward wall at a table with Bill. Crawford began working his way along toward them.

Bill saw Jim coming and leaned back. He and Given had been bending close, talking, but the moment Jim joined them they became noncommittal and broodingly silent. He sank down, pushed back his hat, and said: "Cuff Banning's startin' his gather." They both looked

116

at him like he'd just said night follows day. He tried again. "All right, so Colin's organizing his drive to go south. I'm in favor of gettin' up a big armed posse from here in town, goin' out to their gatherin' grounds, and makin' a big arrest."

That did it. Bill Haines's expression turned mildly agonized. He pushed his empty glass and the bottle atop their table across in front of Crawford and growled: "Here, wash those boyhood notions out of your skull."

Jim reached to fill the glass. "How else?" he demanded. "And what's the point in prolonging this? If Colin takes a notion to leave the country with all that money, we're goin' to look awful silly, and, if folks ever find out we knew all along, an' he *still* got away, they're goin' to tar and feather all three of us."

"It's not just Colin," muttered Bill, staring at his hands atop the table. "It's also Charley."

Crawford tossed off his drink and straightened in the chair, pushing the bottle and glass over in front of Ed Given.

Still staring at his hands, Haines said: "If we find the money on Colin an' his men, we can make it stick. But what'll we use as proof against Charley?"

Jim thought a moment. Given was staring across the table at him, expressionless and silent. This stare made Jim uncomfortable. He didn't want to appear foolish in front of the ex-lawman. He shrugged, deciding to let the older men have their say, and they did, but the moment Bill began speaking again, Jim understood why Bill was looking so bitter and remorseful.

117

"Ed wants me to take money down and put it in Charley's safe. It's got to be enough money to tempt Charley again." Haines kept glowering at his outstretched hands. "Seven thousand dollars, Jim."

Crawford was both astonished and alarmed. In the first place, the risk held him stiffly in the chair. In the second place, he marveled that Bill still had that kind of money after the other robbery. He finally raised his eyes to Given and saw in the former lawman's eyes an ironic expression. Given seemed to be laughing at Crawford without moving his lips.

Jim reached for the bottle and glass again. Given watched a moment, then said: "It's not just O'Brien, Deputy. Not by a long sight. O'Brien's never going to reach rail's end with those Swallowtail cattle. We know that, because we're going to ambush him before he even gets close. But we're also going to be a long way from town when that happens, and meanwhile . . . Deems can't be left loose back here in Younger. He's got to be under lock and key . . . and guard . . . at our jail house, with a charge filed against him that'll stick. You understand?"

Crawford ultimately said: "I understand, Marshal. But what about Bill, does *he* understand?"

Given's ironic look deepened as he swung to look at scowling Bill Haines. "Sure, Bill understands." Then Given lowered his voice and murmured: "Bill's worth seven thousand dollars." The way he said that put Jim in mind, not of Bill's accumulated wealth, but rather of a $7,000 reward.

Haines reached for the bottle. After he'd downed a big one, he glared and said: "Given, I ought to shoot you. I ought to have shot you the first day I found out who you were."

"It's not too late now to try it," murmured the ex-lawman.

Bill shook his head. "When a man takes off his gun, he gets rusty. No. I wouldn't stand the chance of a snowball in hell. But just the same . . . I should've done it. *Tried* it, anyway. You're goin' to lose my last seven thousand for me, sure as God made green apples."

Given shook his head. "I don't think so, Bill. Besides, you're goin' to be with the deputy and me when we stake out Charley Deems."

"Oh, no!" exclaimed Haines. "You rode me all over the lousy countryside once . . . for nothing. You don't get me into another of your schemes."

But Bill didn't sound at all convincing. That $7,000 had taken a long time to acquire. Jim could see Bill's resolve evaporating before his eyes. Bill would be along. He wouldn't like it, but he'd be along.

CHAPTER
EIGHT

The next morning Bill Haines took his $7,000 down and deposited it at the general store in Charley Deems's safe. The same day, but somewhat later, Jim entered the Territorial Saloon and met Given there having a glass of malt liquor. Given seemed tickled about something, but the only way Jim could be sure of this was the manner Given showed, quite different from his usual crisp, unsmiling attitude.

"Bill put the money in Deems's safe, Deputy. He's in the backroom now, oiling a gun he hasn't worn in a long time, so, if you want a drink, you'll have to go behind the bar and get it yourself."

Jim didn't want a drink. He said: "Marshal, what's the plan?"

"We take turns watching the store from your jail house, Deputy, unless you know of some way we can get still closer to that safe."

"You figure Charley's going to take it by himself this time?"

"I think he's *got* to take it by himself, Deputy. O'Brien's got bigger fish to fry. By my estimate he's driving over four thousand head. That much beef represents a lot more than any lousy seven thousand dollars. Besides, O'Brien's not foolish enough to come back here, unless he can do it late at night, and I just can't see a smart man like O'Brien taking that long a chance for what he could perhaps get out of it, when he's already got a sure thing." Given turned and leaned on the bar. "The morning stage went through several hours ago. I sent a letter to your boss over at the county seat. I'm tellin' you this because I don't want you to think I'm sticking my nose into your business. I asked the sheriff to wire the owners of Swallowtail Ranch for permission to halt that drive on the grounds that we suspect O'Brien of planning to sell the beef and pocket the money. I also asked the sheriff to get the reply back to us here at Younger the same day it arrives, if he can do it."

Jim saw Bill Haines emerging from a distant doorway. He rapped his knuckles on the bar and called for Bill to fetch him a drink. Then he said: "Marshal, why all the legalities?"

"Deputy, up to now O'Brien's been legally selling Swallowtail beef. He's had the authority. Down at rail's end the buyers won't question him now any more than they have in the past. We need a stop order. We can't just ride in and tell those buyers they can't take that beef. Since this town at rail's end isn't even in your county, that badge you wear isn't any good."

Bill brought the drink, and Crawford downed it. As he replaced the glass, he saw the saw-handle black rubber butt of a six-gun strapped to the barman's right hip. He looked a moment, then looked away. Haines was belligerently scowling; he wore the gun self-consciously and expected some comment. Crawford wisely made none.

121

"Well," said Given, waiting for Jim to make some comment.

Jim did. He said quietly: "Got to hand it to you, Marshal. You sure think ahead. All right. What's next?"

"Starting tonight we stake out the general store. I'll take first watch. You'll take second. And Bill will keep watch until sunup."

Haines muttered something that sounded blisteringly indecent under his breath but Jim ignored it since he couldn't understand it anyway. "How about the Swallowtail drive? It ought to be under way by now. How long can we fool around here with Charley?"

Given lifted his shoulders, dropped them, and rapped the bar top for a drink. Bill reached back for a fresh bottle, looking unhappy. "From here on," said Given, "we play them as they're dealt. With a lot of luck we ought to be able to sock Deems away by tomorrow. He knows by now that O'Brien's moving the cattle. He'll also know that he's got to join O'Brien soon or lose out on his cut of the fourteen thousand. Care for a drink, Bill?"

Haines glowered but he drank, then he softly belched, leaned far over in front of Crawford, and said: "Jim, I got somethin' to tell you. I don't 'specially *want* to tell you, but that's how things go sometimes. A feller does foolish things an' eventually they come back an' haunt him." Haines paused, leaned harder, and peered upward from beneath shaggy brows. "Years back I . . . well . . . I roped a few horses in Missouri that belonged to other folks."

Jim waited. There was to be more; he could tell that from the way Given was watching Haines, and also from Bill's contorted face. It didn't really come as any surprise to Crawford; he'd come to suspect something like that lay between these two older men. What he'd had no inkling about were, of course, the actual details.

"And there was a shooting scrape down in New Mexico Territory, Jim, when Ed Given here was the law down there. It wasn't murder, but still, if I'd been on the right side of the law, it probably wouldn't have ended up in a gunfight. Afterward, with Given an' others ridin' right behind, I made for California. I lost 'em in San Francisco an' came on up into Oregon. I quit runnin' when I found this town." Haines stopped, kept peering upward from beneath his brows, and finally said quietly: "Given knew me right off. I figured he would because he had that kind of reputation in Kansas an' also in New Mexico."

Crawford reached for the bottle. "But Marshal Given's retired now, Bill, and me . . . well, I'm just a sort of cowboy turned deputy sheriff. I got all the worry I need right here in Younger. Besides, if we all come through this mess with Colin O'Brien and Charley Deems, I sort of figure we'll have pretty well squared a lot of accounts." Crawford carefully filled all three glasses, corked the bottle, and set it aside. As he reached for his glass, he said: "You know, Bill, I haven't always been exactly any angel myself. One time down in Arkansas . . ." He lifted the glass and slowly smiled. "We been pretty good friends, Bill. On top of that I got probably the lousiest memory in Oregon."

Given lifted his glass. So did Bill Haines. They drank, put down the glasses, and were solemn for a moment. At the door two cowboys stamped inside, laughing. It was a jarring sound at such a time. Haines straightened up off the bar to go serve them. Given gazed at Deputy Crawford.

"How long does a man have to go on paying?" he asked. Then he answered his own question. "When you've been at the trade as long as I was, Deputy, it begins to stick in your craw a little ... the relentlessness of the law. Maybe it's just your age, but sometimes I've gotten sick of pushing men and pushing them until, just to stay alive, they get pushed right into using their guns again."

"I reckon," murmured Jim. "Bill's been one of our town councilmen for a long time. He's sort of gruff at times, but I can tell you for a fact he's overlooked a lot that's been owed him. And that's kind of odd, too ... because so has Charley Deems."

"Yeah," agreed Given. "And that's where the difference comes in, Deputy. One does it because he can remember his own days of want, while the other one does it because hungry people aren't important to him, he's got something a lot bigger in the back of his mind. Well, it's getting' along toward suppertime. I've got to find Rusty and take him to eat. I'll meet you over at the jail house after dark." Given backed off the bar. "Go have a talk with Deems, Deputy. Let him see you around ... let him think you're demoralized by your lack of luck at catching O'Brien. Make it good. I figure he's got a go-between he'll use to send word to O'Brien. Good luck."

Crawford twisted to watch the short, burly ex-lawman leave the saloon. When he straightened back around, Bill was standing across the bar from him, also looking doorward, but Bill's expression was less admiring and more brooding. "Care for another shot?" he asked mechanically. When Jim shook his head, Bill said: "You know, they don't make lawmen like Given any more. He could out-guess a rustler an' out-shoot a gunfighter."

"I thought he *was* a gunfighter when he first hit town, Bill, an' I don't mind tellin' you I was sweatin' a little. I'm fair with a Forty-Five but not in his class."

"Damn' few are, Jim. With a gun or with just plain old cow savvy."

Crawford left the saloon and went along to Agatha Beeman's boarding house to take a bath and change clothes. It was Saturday.

He was just leaving the house, later, when he spied Given and Rusty Miller walking side-by-side down toward the café. He also saw something else, a horseman emerging from around back of town through the eastward alleyway that ran down behind Charley Deems's store, and even at that distance he would have taken an oath it was one of those same Swallowtail cowboys Given had forced into the street brawl with a couple of Cuff Banning's boys a week earlier.

He stood motionlessly for a while, figuring out the probable purpose of that range man being in town. It struck him hard that Charley might have told the cowboy of Bill Haines's $7,000 in Charley's safe. He started southward at a brisk pace. Given had suggested that he let Charley know he was still around. He now meant to do exactly that. As for making Charley think he was demoralized, as Given had also suggested, he thought he might have a little trouble doing that. He'd never been a very good actor.

Given and the lad disappeared into the café without ever seeing Deputy Crawford behind them. Next door was the general store, Jim's destination. There were a few late shoppers inside when Crawford passed in out of the fading daylight and Charley was in the act of lighting a coal-oil lamp. He saw Jim and gravely nodded, then went on with what he was doing. Jim strolled around. Through a front window he could see his jail house. By turning completely around he could also see Charley's big iron safe over in its dingy corner.

Cliffy Hart was stumping along on his way to the same café where Given had also gone. Cliffy didn't look up or he'd have spied Jim in the window of the general store. Two cowboys loped past southward, bound out of town, and a top buggy came swirling in from the same direction. It was the local doctor. Jim wondered where he'd been. He remembered that the doctor, because he was also undertaker, had buried that slain outlaw, and made a mental note to render a bill for that planting to the town council in order to pay the doctor. The fee was static unless the unknown deceased left behind a worthwhile horse or saddle, which in this case he had not; therefore, the town owed the doctor $15, which included having someone read a few words over the grave.

Charley made change for his last customer and walked over. Jim turned only his head to look downward. Charley took out a big red bandanna, and mopped his face.

"Mighty warm for a spring evening," he said. "Going to be a hot summer."

Jim thought of a good answer to that but didn't say it. Bruce Horn went up the yonder sidewalk from his blacksmith shop, walking in a crabbed forward manner as though the bandage beneath his shirt cramped him.

"Good to see him up and around," mused Crawford. "A few inches more to the right an' I reckon he'd be dead, too."

"Too?"

"Yeah. Like that one Cliffy shot."

"Oh, him. Yeah. That's right. Jim, what progress you making?"

Jim rocked back on his heels and turned back to gazing out the window. He didn't want to be looking at Charley when he told the lie. "None. Seems like Colin upped and flew away. Cuff tracked him to a bed of glass rock, but after that he disappeared into thin air."

"Jim, folks come in here every day complainin' that you're not lookin' hard enough." Charley gave his shoulder a little hitch. "I'm not sayin' that, mind you. But you can't blame folks when they lost that kind of money."

"I don't blame 'em," muttered Crawford, still staring straight ahead so that all Deems could see was his profile. "But I can't manufacture their money back for 'em, either. There's just so much a deputy sheriff can do, Charley."

"Sure. I understand," sympathized the merchant, also gazing out the window where dusk was settling over the distant forests and mountains. "Haven't you found *anything?*"

"Nothing, Charley. Not a damned thing. By now I'm almost afraid to tell the sheriff to get out posters on Colin. He'll be leggin' it over the Mex line."

"You haven't reported it to the sheriff yet, Jim?" asked Charley, looking astonished.

"Hell, Charley, that stage only comes through once a week, you know."

"You should've sent someone to the county seat."

Jim considered this morosely and said nothing for a moment. He turned, put his back to the window, and gazed over at the iron safe. "That lousy box," he growled.

Deems also turned around. He nodded and said: "Don't worry, it'll never happen again. I'm through bankin' folks' money for them. All through."

Jim nodded. "Don't blame you." Then it struck him that the way Deems had said that hadn't rung true. "Suppose someone's got money they want locked up, though. This is the only decent safe in town."

"I don't care. No more goes into that thing. Not a red cent. Not even my own money."

"You mean it's empty now, Charley?"

Deems solemnly inclined his head. "And it's going to stay empty, too," he muttered. He reached around to

128

untie his apron and remove it. "I got to lock up, Jim. Excuse me, will you?"

Jim said that he would and strolled thoughtfully out into the lowering night. A sudden thought made his knees turn to water. That rider he'd seen sneaking out of town — that Swallowtail rider — if there really wasn't any money in Charley's safe, then just possibly, Bill Haines's $7,000 was already gone!

He stepped down off the sidewalk and crossed awkwardly over to his jail house, hoping to find Edward Given there, but hoping not to find Bill there. That had been Bill's money.

CHAPTER
NINE

Given was in the office, smoking. He hadn't lighted the lamp. When Crawford entered, Given said: "I saw you through the window over there. What'd he have to say?"

"Marshal," Jim muttered, "there's hell to pay. I think he's already gotten rid of that seven thousand of Bill's."

Given's cigarette dulled out in the room's total gloom. He leaned against the wall, looking over toward the deputy while Jim told him everything that made him believe Haines's cash had already been stolen. For a few moments afterward Given's cigarette glowed before he punched it out and dropped it.

"I don't think so," he drawled. "No, Deputy, I don't think so. If that money *was* gone, why would Deems still be in town? He's no fool. He knows damned well that, if one more robbery occurs at his place, folks are going to start wondering what should've crossed their minds the other time. No, I think he may have *told* that cowboy the money was in the safe, but I don't believe it's gone yet." Given went across to a little barred window and gazed out it for a while. Jim hung up his hat and took a Winchester out of the wall rack. Given turned as Crawford worked the mechanism of the gun and started loading it. He said: "Deputy, we're going to make a little change in our plans. Bill's going around into the alleyway behind the store."

"You figure Charley'll leave that way?"

"Maybe. But that's not what's bothering me now. If he *did* tell that Swallowtail cowboy about Bill's cash in the safe, then I figure that cowboy'll be back to escort Deems out of town. We can't see around behind the store, so one of us had better make a stakeout over there."

"I could do it, Marshal."

"No. Bill would be much better, Deputy. That's his money, remember."

Haines walked in moments later, carrying a shotgun, one of those traditional weapons bartenders kept under their bars. The barrel had been hacked off so that the weapon wasn't more than three feet long from stock to barrel's end. Its range was limited, but for a distance of 100 feet it threw a pattern of buckshot powerful enough to cut a man in two.

Given told Haines what Crawford had encountered at the store, and Bill's anger boiled over. He swore mightily and vowed no one was going to get his last $7,000. He also said he never should have listened to Given. When the storm subsided and Given suggested that Haines stake out the alleyway over behind the general store, Bill vigorously assented, and once again reiterated his earlier denunciation of the whole scheme from start to finish. He was reaching for the door latch when Crawford offered him a handful of loads for his scatter-gun.

Bill took them and glowered. "Ed Given," he growled, "if that money gets away, I'm going to hold you responsible. And another thing. If Charley and this

Swallowtail rider get past me some way, damned if I'm goin' to go on playin' cat-an'-mouse, either, I'm going after O'Brien myself."

Given stepped over closer to the door and spoke in a low, tough tone of voice. "Bill, you upset this thing and I'll give you a third eye. Now you remember that. One thing we *don't* need right now is a hothead. If those two sneak around you some way, you come back here and we'll all *three* of us go after O'Brien."

After Haines had departed, Jim Crawford blew out a big breath. "He was mad clear through, Marshal. I've seen him roiled up before but never that bad."

Given's answer was laconic. "Odd thing about reformed outlaws, Deputy. They're like preachers who've been drunks and the like. When they get religion, they get all fired up with it, become regular zealots. You know, there was a time when Bill Haines would have stepped aside and wished Deems good luck. Only now, the shoe's on the other foot."

Jim finished loading the carbine and offered it to Given. The ex-lawman pushed it aside, saying he didn't need a carbine. Whatever would happen tonight wouldn't happen at long range.

They began their vigil. When Given suggested that Crawford get some rest so he'd be fresh to take over the watch when his turn came, Jim declined. He wasn't sleepy and, furthermore, he said that he never in his life felt less like lying down.

They shared a smoke and watched the town from Jim's jail house windows. At Haines's saloon men came and went. Someone up there was playing a guitar and a girl was singing. The stores were dark now. A few people were out strolling; it was another warm, perfect evening. Time dragged. Jim made a pot of coffee and Given sipped a cup of it beside the window. They talked a little back and forth, nothing important, just the kind of things men discuss when they're waiting for action. Given spoke mostly of the orphan boy, Rusty Miller. Jim told him all he knew about the lad, which wasn't very much.

"His folks came here as homesteaders, three, four years back, and settled east of town. When an epidemic hit that winter before they had their shack completed, they both got carried off. Since then the kid's been doing odd jobs for Cliffy, for me, for anyone who needed something done. He moved into an old abandoned miner's shack north of town."

"Sounds familiar, that story," murmured Given, gazing across at the general store. "In the East they have foundling homes. Not that they're much better than shifting for yourself, still, a boy gets three meals a day." Given finished the coffee, turned, and put the cup aside. "Well, I reckon that'll work itself out, Deputy. I need someone to help me fish and hunt and build a cabin. Rusty's about right for it." Given resumed his watching. "Raise a few horses maybe and some cattle. A boy ought to learn more than just how to shoot."

"Yeah."

They watched the hitch rack up at the Territorial begin to lose most of its saddle horses as the night ran on. A little after midnight the last range rider pulled out and Bill's hired barman doused the lights and barred the door. The only lights still showing along the roadway, after that, came from a pair of smoking carriage lamps bolted to either side of the roadway entrance of Cliffy's barn. Crawford regarded those lights for a while, then said: "I've told the old coot a hundred times that's a pure waste of coal oil. As well try to reason with a stone, though. Cliffy's the hardest-headed feller I've ever run across."

"But a good shot," murmured Given.

Jim ran that through his mind. "I'll say it again . . . I had no idea he could shoot, Marshal. At least not that good."

"Never can tell about those old-timers, Deputy. I'd guess Cliffy Hart's been other things beside a liveryman in his time."

Jim looked over at Given but it was too dark to ascertain the expression there, so he returned to leaning against a wall, watching the yonder roadway. He thought he saw a small flicker of light and rubbed his eyes. It was gone. "Reflection off the window," he muttered. Given either didn't hear that or was thinking of something else, for he didn't ask Jim to repeat it.

Jim straightened up. That couldn't have been a reflection on Charley's front window. The only lights showing now were up at Cliffy's barn, which was too far northward to cast reflections this far south. "Marshal," he said, "I thought I saw a light over in the store."

Given leaned closer. So did Crawford. For a while there wasn't a sound or a light. Then it came again, soft

134

and shielded as though it came from a candle and not a lamp.

"There it is again, Marshal."

Given said softly: "I see it. Deputy, open the door. Don't go out, just open the door. And be quiet about it."

Jim moved to obey. As he was doing this, Given muttered something under his breath, swept his right hand downward, and stepped swiftly over toward the doorway opening. He'd obviously seen that faint brightness again.

Jim said breathlessly: "You see it?"

Given was in the doorway before he replied. "Yeah. Listen, now. You walk out of here and watch the front roadway. If Bill's in place, the back will be under surveillance. I'm going across and see if I can spot anyone inside through the window."

"Be damned careful. They can background you."

Given stepped out of the office, gun in hand. There was no longer any light over there. Crawford moved stealthily out behind him, holding his Winchester in both hands up across his body.

The town was utterly hushed and dark except for those livery barn lamps up the northward roadway. Given moved without a sound through the roadway dust. Crawford watched him so intently he forgot also to watch the roadway.

Given stepped up onto the far sidewalk, moved off to the left a little, and crouched forward to peer into the store window. A roaring blast of gunfire broke out. Crawford saw Given drop like stone and started to

135

move, but the window over there was still intact. There was another of those thunderous blasts. Given rolled, jumped up, and called out to Crawford as he raced northward to the first narrow passageway. Crawford saw him disappear through that dark little place and raced for it himself.

Some dog started barking through town and somewhere a window banged as it was abruptly slammed open. A man's startled voice made a high, shrill bleat over in the alleyway. Crawford saw Given spring out through the exit into the yonder alleyway and worked his own way down there, too. Then he heard Bill Haines's profanity above all the other sounds, jumped out clear of the dogtrot, and swung his carbine. Northward came the sounds of a shod horse, fleeing in high panic.

"Don't shoot, don't shoot!" Charley Deems was wailing over and over. "I surrender, don't shoot!"

Haines was standing in the pale starlight with his legs wide-spread and his sawed off shotgun in both hands. He'd evidently reloaded the thing because he had it pointing straight at Charley where the storekeeper was straining back against the rear wall of his own store.

"Shoot," snarled Bill, stiff with outrage. "I ought to blow you in two, you lousy double-dealin' thief, you!"

Given wasn't paying any attention to those two. He was standing above a sprawled, dark form in the center of the alley. As Crawford watched, Given put up his .45 and knelt. Crawford walked over, still holding his Winchester.

136

Given looked up. "You got a match?" he quietly asked. Jim rummaged, found one, and struck it. He and Given bent closer to look into the face of the dead man. Given said: "Thought so. This one I recognize. He's one of them."

The match went out, and Jim dropped it. "He's one of that pair you made fight Banning's boys last week. I think he's the same one I saw loping out of town earlier tonight."

Given got up and dusted his knee. "Sure wasn't watching tonight, though," he muttered. "That buckshot caught him head on."

They turned and went over to where Bill was still holding Charley Deems pinned to the wall with his scatter-gun. Bill's face was a mask of deadly wrath. Given put out a hand and gently forced the shotgun down. To Bill he said: "It's all over. Relax."

Bill lowered the gun but he didn't relax. In fact, he didn't take his furious glare off Deems until Given got between them. Deems seemed to be scarcely breathing; his face was as gray as putty.

"Where's the money?" Given asked, pushing out his hand.

Charley gulped and forced himself to look away from Bill Haines. "In my shirt," he croaked. "Inside my shirt. Keep him away from me. Jim . . . Deputy Crawford . . . don't let him —"

Given stepped closer and tore the shirt, interrupting Deems's words. He drew forth a black leather wallet that was tightly wound around with a length of cord. The wallet bulged with Bill Haines's $7,000. Given

137

turned and handed the wallet to Bill. "Count it," he said. Crawford reached out for Bill's shotgun, which Haines relinquished in order to tear at the cord on the wallet.

Given frisked Deems, found no weapons, and said: "You aren't as smart as folks think you are. That man out there in the road, did he come here to help you with the robbery?"

"No. No, he came to ride out of town with me. He was in town earlier ..." Deems snapped his jaws closed, but Given shook his head at him.

"No need to try and hide anything now," he stated. "We know all of it, Deems. He came in earlier to tell you how far south O'Brien was with the herd. You told him about the seven thousand and asked him to come back tonight. He did ... and there he lies, shot full of buckshot and deader than a mackerel."

"It's all here," Bill growled, stuffing the wallet into his coat pocket and looking slightly less savage. "I saw that dead one ride up the alley. He was leadin' another horse. I waited until he went inside, then moved over closer to the back door. When the pair of them snuck out a few minutes later, I called on 'em to stop. That damned fool went for his gun. I was already cocked and aimed, so I let him have it. His horse broke loose an' ran an' Charley let out a squawk. I figured he was goin' for a gun, too, so I swung around and tugged off the other barrel, but I missed. I don't know how I ever missed at that range, but I sure did. Then Charley commenced screamin' that he surrenders an' I couldn't shoot him because I had to reload."

138

Crawford walked up and tugged Deems off the wall. Charley came away, walking like he was going to collapse any second. Neither of them said anything as they started down the alleyway toward the nearest intersecting roadway on their way around to the jail house.

Given went back and took another long look at the dead outlaw. He turned suddenly and called to Bill. Haines stamped over, still stiff with indignation. "He's dead, isn't he?" Bill querulously asked. "Hell, Ed, I give him the full barrel right in the brisket."

"He's dead, Bill, sure. That's not what's bothering me."

"Well. What is then? We got Charley. I got back my seven . . ."

"Bill. His horse. You said it got clear."

"It did. What of that?"

"Use your head. That damned horse'll head for O'Brien's camp as straight as an arrow. There'll be blood on it!"

Bill's eyes gradually opened wide. He breathed a soft curse. "Come on, damn it. We got to get Jim and beat that horse to O'Brien. *Come on!*"

CHAPTER
TEN

Jim was writing in his office log when Haines and Given burst in. He put aside the pen and closed the book with pleased finality. "He's lodged under grand theft. That'll hold him until the cows come home. But that's only the start of it. I'll —"

"Get your hat," Given snapped. "That outlaw's horse is heading for O'Brien's camp with blood on its saddle. We've got to catch the critter, cut it off, or else make a stab at taking O'Brien himself. The minute he sees that bloody saddle he's going to figure out that something's wrong. With fourteen thousand in his money belt, he's not going to stay with the herd. Fourteen thousand and a live pelt's going to look a lot better to him than five times that much and a grave."

Crawford sprang up, seized his hat, his Winchester, and ran out of the office behind Given and Bill Haines. They got to Cliffy's barn in a rush, scattered to saddle up, and weren't aware that they were not alone until someone cocked a gun in the murky runway. That little unmistakable sound froze them all.

Old Cliffy's voice shrilled from a far corner. "Horse thieves, eh? I heard that shootin' over across the road. So you fellers figured you'd rush in here and steal some horses, did you? Well, let me tell you . . . one move and I'll . . ."

"Cliffy, dammit!" exclaimed Jim Crawford. "Put up that gun. This is Jim. Jim Crawford. These other two fellers are Bill Haines and Marshal Given. Cliffy, confound it, light a lamp or something. We haven't got a minute to spare."

Bill Haines said: "Cliffy, you old coot, if you don't uncock that gun, I'm going to take it away from you and ram it . . ."

"Bill? Jim Crawford?" the old man cried out. "What the hell's going on?"

"No time to explain right now," said Given, turning back to rigging out the first horse he'd found. "Deems over at the general store was in on that other robbery with O'Brien. Tonight he tried to steal another seven thousand."

"Mine," snarled Bill Haines.

"I'll pay for the horse when I get back," Given went on. "But right now we've got to reach O'Brien's camp before a horse packing a bloody saddle gets there." Given swung up.

Twenty feet away Jim was frantically bitting up. Bill Haines, already bitted, was fumbling with an elusive latigo. Given whirled out of the barn and swung to the left, up the roadway. Behind him Crawford came next. When Bill came, he was holding a latigo end in one hand and helplessly cursing. He hadn't gotten the latigo knot tied and was forced now to ride holding the thing tightly, otherwise it would work loose and permit his saddle to turn.

Cliffy trotted out to the sidewalk and craned around, still holding his .45 and muttering to himself. He remained like that for only a moment, though, then shoved the six-gun into his waistband and went skipping back inside to saddle himself a horse. Because he knew every move and never wasted a second, he was ready to ride by the time the other three had cut westward out of town and were racing through the dingy night. He had his boots and trousers on, but his long nightshirt flapped, held in at the middle by his gun belt. When he raced southward down the empty roadway, a few men, also awakened and brought outside by curiosity, gaped. Cliffy went flapping past like a ghost.

He had been right in one thing; the sounds of the other three had passed down the land bearing southward outside of town. That had been Given's idea. Given had yelled it to the others.

"Follow the road. We'll make better time and maybe get ahead of the horse."

They sped along through the still night with little more than instinct to guide them. The roadway was flanked on both sides by trees, but enough pale starlight shone to permit some visibility. For a mile or better they rode like this, then Given stopped and sprang down to put his ear to the ground. This permitted Bill also to jump down and tighten the latigo. They were away again a moment later. Jim hollered over, asking if Given had caught any sounds from the earth. Given replied that he had not.

They repeated this same procedure farther along and Given still heard nothing. Finally they had to slacken off in order to favor their winded mounts. Not until then did Bill say he thought they should have by this time at least caught some sight or sound of the runaway horse.

Jim concurred. "We've covered more miles than a loose horse ordinarily would. My guess is that the critter either took to the trees, in which case he probably returned to the ranch, or else he's behind us somewhere, stopping for a blow."

Given neither agreed nor disagreed. He simply kept on riding southward. Bill Haines finally asked him where he thought they might come onto the Swallowtail herd. Given had a specific answer for that.

"Twelve miles south of Younger and two miles west."

Haines's eyebrows shot up. "How do you know that?" he inquired.

"Rusty," stated Given, and volunteered nothing more.

They kept their animals at a swift walk for almost an hour, then loped again. This time, because the gait was less punishing, they were able to keep to it longer. When Given ultimately drew down to a walk again, he asked Jim Crawford where, southward, drovers usually made their camps down in this country. There had to be both feed and water, but in summertime Oregon this was never much of a problem; the thing was, which of the many available places were traditionally used.

Jim mentioned several places by local names. He'd cowboyed this country, he said, when he'd first come to the state. He also said, if they now left the road and bore off westerly down through the thinning trees, they'd either scent as big a drive as O'Brien had organized, or possibly even hear it.

Given and Haines let Crawford take the lead from here on. They spoke a little as they rode and Bill felt for his wallet every now and then as though carrying all that money on his person made him uneasy, which it did.

"Suppose there's a fight," he finally blurted out, "and I stop one. I got all this cash on me, Given."

The ex-lawman looked around and gravely said: "Bill, if you're only wounded, what the doctors don't cheat you out of, I'll keep for you. But if you're killed . . . why, if I were you, damned if I'd take off without it."

"Thanks," growled Haines. "You're a big help."

Jim led them down to a wide, shallow creek where they watered the horses, had a cigarette, and noticed that the eastward horizon was pinkly brightening. As they started on again, Given smoked and furrowed his brows in thought. They were well away from the creek before he said what was on his mind.

"Deputy, I think you're right. We should've seen that horse by now, at least his tracks, if he was ahead of us. I don't think he lit out for this camp down here. I think he probably ran back to the ranch, where he was possibly raised or where at least he's been fed for a few years."

Crawford agreed with this and said so. He also said, unless Given particularly wished to see where the Swallowtail herd was, he thought the three of them should turn back, round up Cuff Banning's riders and perhaps some others, then come back for the showdown with the Swallowtail crew.

144

Given disagreed. His reasons were logical. "Whether that horse goes to the cow camp or not, Deputy, O'Brien's going to miss that man Bill killed in the back alley. He may send a rider back to see what's going on, or he may not, but one thing is certain. O'Brien's going to be almighty spooky from now on. We can't take another chance on him getting away."

Bill concurred. "If one of Colin's men rides into town, hears there's a dead Swallowtail rider in Doc's embalmin' shed and also hears Charley Deems is in jail, he's going to have to be awful dumb not to figure out something went wrong, and beat it fast down here to tell Colin. No, Jim, like I've said before . . . Given's right. He doesn't make a whole lot of mistakes."

Crawford had only advanced a suggestion; he wasn't married to it. When the other, older men voted it down, he rode along content to conform.

It was near dawn when Jim, several hundred feet ahead making a little scout around an open glade, heard a horse and swung frantically to beckon Given and Haines on up closer. The three of them dismounted and listened. The beast was plodding along from the west. It was difficult to tell yet whether it was the loose animal they sought or perhaps a horse with a man on its back. Given motioned for silence and crept off through the trees. He wasn't gone long, and, when he returned, he flagged his companions forward, told them it was a ridden horse, and gestured for them to fan out.

By this time the oncoming rider was occasionally visible where he moved in and out of tree shadow.

Given was directly in front of him. Haines was off to his right, Crawford off to his left. The rider evidently suspected nothing. He came on, acting bored or indifferent or drowsy until Given stepped out into sight and the horse, seeing Given first, snorted and sucked back into a stiff-legged halt which flung the rider up against the swells of his saddle. At once the man's right arm started downward. Given stopped it.

"Hold it, mister. Just hold it."

The cowboy's hand ceased to move. He squinted at Given a little irritably. "You got nothin' better to do with your time than jump out at folks?" he growled. "That's an awful good way to die young."

Given had his hand lightly lying upon his .45 but he made no additional move to draw it. "Who are you?" he asked, and got back another irritable answer.

"What's it to you? I could ask you the same question."

Bill Haines stepped forth, looking thunderous. "Answer," Bill snarled, "or I'll yank you off that saddle and pound some manners into you!"

Jim Crawford came up on the cowboy's other side. The cowboy looked from one to the other, then back to Given. Now his face was mirroring astonishment and apprehension rather than annoyance. "My name's Jared Cooper. I ranch about six miles west o' here an' I'm eastbound to see a neighbor about some critters I can't seem to find on my range. I figured they might have strayed over onto —"

"All right," Given interrupted him. "Have you seen a big drive passing southward or any sign of one?"

146

Jared Cooper, gazing grimly at Jim Crawford who he seemed half to recognize, nodded. "Swallowtail," he said. "Yeah. They went through yesterday morning real early. I heard 'em an' rode out to see who it was."

"Do you know Swallowtail's range boss, Colin O'Brien?"

"Yes, but he wasn't with the herd. All the other fellers was along, but O'Brien wasn't. At least I didn't see him. Funny thing, too, they didn't have their bedroll wagon along. I never seen Swallowtail, or any other big outfit, either, for that matter trail down to rail's end without havin' a wagon along to haul their grub and such like." The rancher paused long enough to rear back a little in his saddle and squint straight at Crawford. "Say, aren't you the deputy from up around Younger?"

Jim said that he was and asked if Jared Cooper had heard anything about a robbery at Younger. Cooper shook his head. He hadn't been in town in five weeks, he said, and didn't expect to go there for another five weeks, providing his flour and cornmeal held out. Then, while he spoke, Cooper's brow began to crease; his eyes began to draw out narrowly as he seemed mentally to sniff around the implications here. "Are you boys sayin' Colin O'Brien's mixed up in a robbery?" he asked.

Bill Haines put up his gun. Crawford lowered his carbine. They looked at Given, who jerked his head. The three of them turned and hastened back to the horses, leaving Jared Cooper staring after them, completely nonplussed.

"Can't be too far ahead," Crawford opined as they rode on, holding to their southwestward course. "Fat cattle move slow and you can't even stampede 'em in forested country."

Bill Haines suddenly chuckled. "You see the look on that feller's face when he saw all three of us with guns? He'll eat his heart out until he gets to a town to find out what's going on."

Given twisted in the saddle suddenly, cocked his head, then said: "Maybe, Bill. And maybe he'll come ridin' after us. Listen."

They heard the horse coming and coming fast. Crawford said this one had also to be a ridden horse; it was weaving through the trees like any horse would do, but unlike a riderless horse it was also holding steadily to a constant course, which happened to be right down the tracks Given and Crawford and Haines were making.

They spread out again, this time remaining in their saddles. Given and Jim Crawford took the west side and Bill Haines faded out on the east side of their trail. They sighted something up through the trees but it didn't look like any range rider any of them had ever seen before. Crawford raised his carbine and waited. Haines, over across a little intervening distance, removed his hat, furiously scratched his head, and resettled the hat. Edward Given strained to make out whatever it was that was plunging straight on toward them.

Crawford suddenly lowered the Winchester. His mouth dropped a foot. "No," he croaked at Given. "It couldn't be. It just couldn't be."

But it was.

Bill Haines recognized the old man, too, and jumped his horse out to block Cliffy's rush. As soon as Cliffy set back, he also recognized Haines and made a big, wide grin at him. Haines did not grin back. Neither did Given nor Jim Crawford; they simply urged their mounts out and sat there, staring at the liveryman, who was girded at the middle with a very business-like gun and shell belt, but who was otherwise uniquely attired in a pink-striped, ankle length nightshirt that was hoisted above his knees.

"What in the hell do you think you're doing, Cliffy?" demanded Haines.

"Lookin' for you fellers. What'd you think I was doin'? Where's them consarned outlaws? Lead me to 'em!"

CHAPTER
ELEVEN

Bill Haines angrily ordered Cliffy to go back. The old man sat up there, stiff as a poker and defied Haines, defied all three of them in fact, and said he was going along, too.

Given shrugged and looked at the others. "We don't have much choice unless we want to sit here arguing all day."

So they rode along with old Cliffy chirping happily in their midst, his ridiculous attire as out of place as a man's clothing — or lack of it — ever had been.

But it turned out a mile farther along that old Cliffy knew this southward country better even than Jim Crawford did. He pointed westward after Haines had reluctantly told him why they were down here, saying that the bed grounds used by most of the big outfits were off in that direction. Then he proceeded to lead them inland to prove that he knew what he was talking about.

They cut the sign of the Swallowtail herd just as the sun came up, found where a night camp had been made, and paused there while old Cliffy went sniffing around, bent half over, peering intently at the ground, his pink-striped nightshirt flapping around his booted trouser legs. Bill Haines, standing beside his horse at the cool ashes, curled his lips.

"If that's not the silliest looking get-up I ever saw on a grown man, I'll put in with you."

Given and Jim Crawford, feeling the ashes and kneeling, didn't look around. They knew what Haines meant. They also knew Haines was still irritated by Cliffy's presence.

They were ready to ride southward again on the well-marked trail when Cliffy came over, leading his horse and looking solemn. "Mister," he said to Given, "seeing as how you're sort of the leader, I got something to tell you."

"Save it an' get on your horse," growled Bill Haines. "Hurry up, Cliffy. You said you weren't going to slow us down if we let you come along. Now get astride and talk . . . if you just *got* to talk . . . while we're riding."

Cliffy politely waited for Bill to stop. He didn't look at Haines, though, but kept gazing straight up at Given. He said: "If that whiskey-swillin' pardner of yours'll shut up for a minute, mister, I'd like to show you something."

Bill exploded. He even started to pile down off his horse, but Jim Crawford caught him in an iron grip and pushed Bill upright in the saddle. "You try that again," Jim drawled without smiling, "and Bill . . . you'll get all the scrappin' you'll want for an awful long time."

Bill glared but he controlled himself. Given, gazing at Cliffy, dismounted without a word and walked off with the liveryman. They halted out where some boot tracks showed, going and coming. Cliffy walked back farther and showed where a horse had been tied back in the trees. He then led Given still farther back and showed

151

him a fresh shod-horse trail leading straight west. Finally the old man turned, put both hands on his hips, and said: "Mister, I'm a sight older'n you are, which means maybe my eyes aren't so good an' my wits aren't as quick, but I'll tell you one thing. I was readin' sign, redskin and whiteskin, when you was trottin' around in three-cornered pants, and those tracks are as plain to me as the pages of a book. Plainer because I can't read a book."

Given looked at the tracks, and looked back at the old man. "What do they say?" he asked.

"One man, mister, one man come ridin' in from the west by hisself. He come after dark an' he come real slow and sly-like. He hid his horse and snuck up to the camp, probably ate supper, visited a spell, then snuck back, got on the horse, and rode away westward again. He done all that slow and real careful."

Given gazed at Cliffy a long time before he turned and went back to the others with Cliffy following after him. "Bill," Given said, "Deputy, I just got a new lease on life. When that rancher back there said that O'Brien wasn't with the drive, my heart sank a yard. I thought he'd already gotten spooked and run off."

"Well . . . ?" growled Bill, bending a black look upon Cliffy.

"He's with the drive, but he's keeping out of sight during daylight just in case. He's paralleling the drive far to the west."

Haines and Crawford sat a moment considering this as Given and old Cliffy got back astride. When the four of them were riding off again, Cliffy said he'd head west

152

and do a little scouting. Given didn't object, Jim Crawford said nothing, and Bill Haines, still miffed at the old man, didn't even bother to turn his head. Cliffy went off through the trees while the other three kept on down the southward trail. Once they surprised a sly old cow that'd obviously hid until the riders had passed by, then had come out, and started back for her home range, grazing leisurely as she passed along. This was not an unusual thing; such critters were called cut-backs. This one wouldn't have aroused much interest, either, except that she was the first Swallowtail animal they had thus far seen, which meant the balance of the herd was not too far ahead. She had a very legible brand in the shape of a swallowtailed pennant on her right side. When she saw the horsemen, they were close enough to head her, if they'd so desired, and she knew it, so she stood out there gently waggling her head at them in a threatening manner, her long, curved horns bright and wicked. They rode on by.

Bill Haines finally put his wallet inside his shirt and tightly buttoned the garment. When he saw Jim watching him, Bill said: "Well, at least if I stop lead, maybe they won't think to look inside my shirt."

"If you stop a bullet, what'll you care whether they get the money or not?" countered Crawford.

The trail was wide and dusty and strong-smelling. There were flies, too, left behind by the big drive. Given asked once how far they'd come and how far ahead the next town was. Crawford said it was still at least fifteen miles to Carter's Meadow, which was where the railroad ended, and he thought they'd probably covered at least twenty miles since leaving Younger the night before.

Where they paused to water the horses beside a creek, Bill said he'd cheerfully give ten dollars for a plate of beef and two big cups of coffee. Instead, he got a cigarette for breakfast.

They'd only been gone from that spot a short while when old Cliffy came riding up toward them from the south. He had evidently scouted all the way around them and come into the trail farther downcountry. Given halted and waited. Cliffy smiled, twisted, and pointed.

"I saw 'em. They're puttin' up a cloud a mile high down there. They're gettin' ready to take their noonday rest."

Jim said: "How far?"

"Four, five miles," replied the liveryman, and reined out of the way as Given started forward again. "You fellers know what you're ridin' into? There's bound to be the full crew with a herd that size, six or seven men . . . and O'Brien."

Haines mumbled a question at Cliffy: "You see any more of his sign?"

"Sure. Where d'you think I went? He's keepin' along with the drive, only west a couple of miles. He's got another feller ridin' with him, too. I saw both their tracks."

"That will be the other one who was in on the robbery at Charley's store," offered Jim.

Given nodded but kept silent.

154

The sun continued to rise; it turned hot and breathless. Given slouched in the saddle. Their horses, cooled-out now and walking placidly along, had entirely recovered from the initial rush. Bill Haines smoked his cigarette down to a nubbin, smashed it against the saddle horn, and tossed it away. He raised both arms and mightily yawned, then he fell to studying the onward land.

The trees this far south of Younger grew larger and broader, but no thicker, which permitted some grass to grow although ordinarily, where pines stood, grass seldom survived the turpentine saturation of the roundabout soil.

Brush also grew, but again, because of the pine trees, it rarely thrived except out where the infrequent clearings appeared. It was in one of these clearings that Cliffy pointed out the tracks of two drag riders following the herd. Given looked and said O'Brien wasn't taking any chances; one drag rider was usually plenty. Two meant that one was watching the drag while the other was watching the back trail.

Near one o'clock they heard cattle. Cliffy faded away again, this time without saying he was going. Bill made a grumbling comment that old Cliffy was going to get caught and upset everything, but Jim Crawford scowled at Haines, saying that the saloon man ought to stop picking on old Cliffy, and Bill had no more to say. The sounds of cattle steadily increased. Given kept his head cocked as he slouched along until the noise seemed reasonably close, then he led the others off to the left and away from the dusty trail. He patently had in mind

155

that, if there were two drag riders, one of them just might, from time to time, lope back a half mile or so looking for pursuers.

They nearly missed Cliffy when he returned from his impromptu scenting that time and Bill growled at the older man not to leave them again. Cliffy said he had no intention of doing that because he'd seen the drag riders less than a mile ahead.

They all straightened in their saddles. Given and Crawford exchanged a look. Jim lifted his shoulders and dropped them, meaning evidently by this that, although he wasn't precisely enthusiastic about the four of them tackling Colin O'Brien and his Swallowtail gun hands, if Given thought it was the thing to be done, he'd go along with it.

Given began making a cigarette, riding with his reins flopping. He said: "Deputy, when a man thinks over all the alternatives to everything in his life, he'll get so upset he won't do anything. I know . . . we started out to keep one horse with a bloody saddle from reaching this bunch. Well, the horse evidently never came this way at all. But we did. And we're here. So . . . the alternatives are to hit 'em or go back. It's an awful long way back." Given lit up, exhaled a gray cloud, and picked up his reins. "Going back wouldn't put us back down here again until maybe day after tomorrow, and I think O'Brien would have the herd sold by then and be . . . the Lord knows where."

Bill Haines was listening. He kept bobbing his head up and down. Jim, seeing this, made a wry little grimace. It was clear enough that Bill didn't think Edward Given was capable of making any mistakes.

They loped for fifteen minutes and finally halted in a grove of oaks with a flat, open stretch of grassland dead ahead where they could distantly make out an enormous moving tide of red backs. The clouds of dust arising from that strolling herd billowed out almost as thick as smoke, but a totally different color.

"This," murmured Given, "changes things. How do we cross this open country without being seen?"

Cliffy chirped right up. "Go west an' around 'em, or wait for nightfall and go right on across the clearing. There isn't any other way."

He was right; even Bill Haines agreed with that. Given seemed satisfied, too. He also seemed thoughtful, but pleased. He got stiffly down from the saddle, stepped on his cigarette to kill it, and watched the others also dismount. "We've made it," he announced. "And we've got a little time to rest and plan. Tell me . . . you boys know the Swallowtail outfit better than I do . . . just how tough are those men up there?"

"Damned tough," growled Haines. "I ought to know. Been serving them drinks a long time. Colin never hired a man who couldn't go bear huntin' with a fly swatter."

Jim Crawford gravely nodded. Cliffy screwed up his face in thought, his snow-white hair rumpled and his unsteady, constantly moving eyes slitted almost out of sight. "Tough," he said. "But tough isn't goin' to be enough, boys. It also takes savvy."

Haines turned and glowered. "I suppose you —" he started to say, but got cut off in mid-breath by Given.

"Let him have his say, Bill. You had yours. Go on, Cliffy."

"Well, like I was fixin' to say, just being tough isn't enough. If we wait until dark, I can slip up there and cut every *cincha* on every saddle, an' with some luck I might even be able to set their horses loose."

"You!" exclaimed Haines. "In that danged nightshirt that stands out like a white sheet? Cliffy, sometimes I wonder about just how much sense you've —"

"Who said I'd be wearin' my nightshirt?" flared the old man. "Let me tell you something, Bill Haines. When I was half your age, I was stealin' horses from Injuns. From *Injuns*, mind you, not dumb homesteaders. When a white man steals horses from Injuns, believe me, sonny . . . that's news!"

"Sonny?" growled Haines. "Where do you get that sonny business, you old owl . . . runnin' around in broad daylight in your consarned nightshirt!"

Cliffy grinned. "Mister," he said to Given, "if I can't cut every girth they got down there, I'll eat my hat. Thirty, forty years back folks used to say . . ." Cliffy's smile faded; his voice trailed off into silence. He was staring at Given as though he'd just remembered something. "Marshal," he muttered. "Did I hear Jim call you . . . Marshal?"

"That was a long time ago," Given replied. "Anyway, Cliffy, if you can put that mob of wolves afoot, I'll be more than willing to forget you're a reformed horse thief."

158

Cliffy got red in the face. He looked around. "Sure hot this afternoon, isn't it?" he innocently observed. Jim Crawford chuckled.

"Is that where you learned to shoot good, Cliffy, stealin' horses?"

"*Humph*, trouble with you young fellers nowadays, you don't have manners. When I was a boy, we never asked no personal questions."

"I reckon you didn't," muttered Haines. "You didn't dare. Every mother's son of you was some kind of a night rider."

Cliffy regarded Bill a moment, on the verge of a retort, but he never said it. He just gently smiled. "We got a couple hours to kill. Suppose I take first watch, an' you lads snooze. I'll wake you up before sundown an' we'll get set for some fun."

Bill leaned back, tilted down his hat, and muttered: "Fun he calls it. We'll all be dead before sunup comes again and he thinks that's funny. And me . . . with seven thousand on my danged corpse. That's so damned funny I could laugh myself into tears. *Humph!*"

Given and Crawford exchanged a wink and also settled back. Old Cliffy got up to look after the horses. After that, he disappeared through the trees.

CHAPTER
TWELVE

It was turning dark when Given awoke with a start. Somewhere, not too distant, he'd heard a gunshot. He rolled up to his feet and swung a kick at the bottom of Bill Haines's boots. Bill came awake profanely, which also awakened Jim Crawford. The three of them were blinking and stiffly moving when a second gunshot sounded, this one from somewhere southward and eastward from them.

Bill said: "Cliffy! Where is the old goat? He's supposed to be standing watch."

"I think that's who's being shot at," grumbled Given as he grabbed up his saddle gun and turned eastward toward the denser forest. "Come on."

They went cautiously, for whoever was hunting old Cliffy was also advancing cautiously, and of the known six or seven men with O'Brien's stolen herd, every man jack of them would also have heard those shots and be just as acutely conscious of some kind of trouble as the men from Younger were.

Once, when Jim came close to Given, he said: "Why didn't he just awaken us in turn like he was supposed to do, instead of tryin' to be a hero all alone?"

Given stepped behind a tree as he answered. "Maybe when we're his age, we'll want to prove something, too, Jim."

160

There never was another shot, but the longer they stayed out looking for Cliffy the more anxious Bill Haines became about their unguarded horses.

"Suppose that old idiot changes course and leads 'em smack dab to our hide-out? Hell, they'll slit his throat, take our animals, and you know how far we'll have to walk?"

A coyote yapped behind them, westward. It yapped several times. Bill was turning in that direction when Given made a low, quick growl of warning. Haines dropped without a sound into a chaparral clump and Jim Crawford took one big step to get behind a red-barked old fir tree.

There were three of them, spread out and carrying Winchesters. They were unshaven, sweaty, and wild-looking. Given didn't recognize any of them but he knew without doubt that he was gazing straight at three Swallowtail cowboys. He palmed his six-gun, ready to throw down the moment those three tense men got within range.

But they never advanced that close. They came together, spoke a little, turned, and started back. They were evidently giving up the search. Given motioned for his companions to stay where they were. He glided forward to follow and make certain the Swallowtail men were not coming back. When he was satisfied on this score, he returned. Bill and Jim were crouching together in Bill's chaparral bush. As Given joined them, Bill said: "I know those three. O'Brien's prize troublemakers. If they'd advanced another hundred yards, we could've taken them by surprise."

Given stood up, tested the forest, jerked his head, and started back westward in the direction they'd earlier heard that yapping coyote. They never found the little animal but, over near the horses, they came upon Cliffy. He was winded and thorn-scratched and more shifty-eyed than ever.

"I done m'best," he said rapidly, before the other three could even open their mouths. "I snuck right up . . . but there was a feller back in the bushes who seen me and fired. I had to run like the devil. They commenced hollerin' and runnin' in every direction with their cussed guns. Thank the Lord it was gettin' dark or they'd have nailed me sure."

"Maybe they should have," mumbled Haines darkly. "Now they know we're back here."

Cliffy emphatically shook his head. "They know *one man* is back here, boys, but I can tell you this . . . didn't any of 'em get close enough to make me out."

"Well," stated Jim Crawford logically, "one man or a hundred, Cliffy, they know they're not alone now, so they'll put out a search party. How long do you expect it'll be, before they find our tracks?"

"Not until daylight tomorrow," stated the old man. "An' maybe by then I'll have another trick to show you."

Bill Haines rolled his eyes and groaned. "Another trick," he mumbled. "Ed, we'd better get astride and get away from this spot. O'Brien's no fool, either, you know. He's got all night to have men stalk around back here."

162

Given agreed with this. They got astride and rode westward. Cliffy led because he was familiar with the new course, but the other three, after Cliffy's recent fiasco, eyed him with a lot less confidence than before. Still, he got them safely away from that spot where they'd rested and into some new country where the trees were immense but were also farther apart.

Jim Crawford knew this country. He and Cliffy discussed the lay of the land. There were some breaks and low hills farther out, it seemed, but neither of them favored going that far off. Cliffy reined in beside Given and asked what plan Given thought would effect the downfall of the cattle thieves. Given had no plan but he'd considered for a while, back there with O'Brien's men stalking through the forest, that, if they could capture the men in the night, it could save bloodshed. He mentioned this now and at once Cliffy was enthusiastically favorable. Bill Haines didn't dissent, but he pointedly said that, if they tried anything like that, they should do it all together, meaning, of course, that Cliffy was not to leave their sight again.

Jim probably had a suggestion to make, but he never got to make it. They were well westward and riding slowly with the lowing of tired cattle around them, southward and eastward, when something up ahead sprang up and crashed through the underbrush with a frightful roar. Haines's horse reacted like a hair-triggered green colt. He bogged his head, bawled once, and bucked as hard and as stiff-legged as he could for twenty feet. The first two jumps Haines's visible face was congealed with purest astonishment. The next two

163

jumps Haines showed alarm, and the last end-swapping big pitch catapulted the bar owner through the air like a bundle of old clothing. Haines struck the earth and bounced. As Jim and Cliffy sprang down to run ahead, Given hooked his horse hard to go racing after Haines's mount. He chased the horse entirely by sound and lost it a mile and a half farther westward, which was a tragedy in several ways. As he turned and rode slowly back toward the others, he heard that big animal that had been startled out of its bed to start all this trouble, crashing away northward making guttural, deep-down growls as it fled. A bear.

Haines was sore and battered and bewildered. He'd had a hard fall but nothing had been broken fortunately. He was a little while recovering, but when he eventually shook his head to clear away the last of the cobwebs, he turned on Cliffy with a snarl of rage.

"You an' your quiet livery horses, I think I'll bust your head or wring your skinny neck, you old . . ."

"Easy," soothed Given, dismounting to kneel with the others. "Any horse might have reacted like that, Bill. You know that."

"I know," snarled Haines, "that Cliffy Hart probably knew that lousy horse'd act like that, and probably came down here an' joined us just to see me get bucked off. I ought to . . . *ouch!* Jim, what in tarnation are you tryin' to do, bust a perfectly good leg?"

Crawford, working Haines's leg carefully, desisted. "Wanted to make certain nothing was broken, Bill. That's all."

"Well, nothing is. Just help me up." They did that and supported Haines until he took several tentative steps, retrieved his hat, crushed it atop his head, and faced around toward them and glared.

Given said: "Bill, your carbine went with the horse. But that's not all. I couldn't catch the critter and by sunup he's sure to smell O'Brien's remuda and drift in where he'll be seen and caught."

Cliffy looked like he might make some retaliatory remark about this, to even things up between him and Bill Haines, but he kept quiet. They all kept quiet while they considered their new predicament. Jim broke the silence after a little while. He said: "Hell, don't look so glum, Bill. It could've been worse. You could've broken a leg or a shoulder when you fell. Anyway, O'Brien knows someone's behind him."

Haines glumly nodded. "Yeah. Only now he'll know it's not just one man. Ed, what do you suggest?"

"That we get away from this spot," said Given. "Come on, you can ride double with me."

Bill was bruised from his fall but he stoically bore the discomfort as they rode away westerly again, four men on three horses, and with one thought uppermost in all their minds. They'd lost the initiative; they'd lost all the advantage of surprise. On top of that, they'd also seriously — perhaps fatally — handicapped themselves. Four men on three horses couldn't even hope to outrun seven men on seven horses.

"The darkness will help," murmured Given, when Cliffy turned back to ask if Given didn't think they should not cut southward. "We've got maybe six hours before they find that damned horse. It's funny, isn't it, we came down here to keep them from finding one loose horse . . . and now we've got to come up with something to keep them from finding another loose horse."

"Funny like a kick in the guts with a pointed boot," muttered Bill Haines. "Real funny."

"Marshal," Jim said, "we're far enough west. I can tell by the sound. If we cut southward now, we can maybe come down the far side of the herd, locate their camp, and hit 'em."

Cliffy vigorously nodded his head. This had been exactly what he'd been about to propose. Given turned his head. "You agree?" he asked Haines. "You up to a little more of this?"

"Hell, yes, I'm up to it. You just put me in sight of another horse, an' I'll do the rest. Better yet . . . put me in pistol range of that critter that bucked me off."

Jim grinned. Even Given's eyes glowed in the descending night. Cliffy turned and started southward. It was not fully night yet, but there was no light to see by excepting the almost useless starshine, so they made slow progress. They had the lowing of bedding-down cattle to guide them; as long as they kept that sound always on their left, they would be traveling in the correct direction.

Cliffy dropped back once to say quietly: "It's down here somewhere I figure O'Brien's hidin'."

They went more quietly after that, but they caught no sight of another rider in the gloom, nor did their mounts indicate they scented another horse.

166

"He's probably over at the camp," murmured Crawford. At about the same time Haines raised one arm to point eastward. He said nothing. He didn't have to. Off through the big trees, now bright, now cut off and dark, was a hot little cooking fire. It seemed less than a half mile to their left and well northward, or behind the bedded cattle.

"Catch 'em eatin'," whispered Haines.

They got down and led their animals forward. Given handed his saddle gun to Bill and drew his six-gun. They eventually left the horses tied in order to prevent the Swallowtail animals from catching their scent and possibly arousing the men around the fire with nickering calls. This seemed to make Bill nervous but he said nothing. They'd advanced perhaps another 300 feet when a man stepped out around an old bull pine and said: "Is that you, Nate?"

Given was out front. He'd just begun to slow before that guard appeared. Behind him the other three were farther back and not quite visible. Quick as a flash Given sang out in a low, muffled way.

"Yeah. Supper ready yet?"

The guard lowered his carbine and leaned upon his tree. "Been ready for fifteen minutes," he retorted. "What'd Colin say?"

"He'll be along," grumbled Given, pacing slowly ahead toward the guard.

"I know that, dammit!" exclaimed the guard. "But what did he say?"

Given was fifty feet away. He muttered under his breath and kept on walking. He had his fisted six-gun behind his back.

The guard swore and said: "Speak out, Nate. You sound like you got a mouth full of mush."

Given was thirty feet away, amply close for the outlaw to see his six-gun even in this poor light. He took two more forward steps, halted, and swung the gun out into plain sight.

The guard was squinting hard through the intervening gloom as though Given somehow did not fit the dimensions of the man for whom the guard had mistaken him. The second that blue-black gun barrel appeared, the guard gasped and gave a start. He struck his Winchester butt first upon the ground, hard. Evidently the gun had been cocked and had either a filed trigger spring or one of those hair-like set triggers, because it detonated.

That furious red orange flash of flame temporarily blinded Given even though the gun had fired straight up, skyward. He dropped and fired at the same time. His slug hit tree bark several inches from the alarmed sentry. The man let off a loud cry and flung himself back behind the tree.

Down at the campfire men sprang up with shouts of alarm. Behind Given his friends, thinking something had happened, ran forward to protect him. He rolled clear and yelled at them to take cover. He sighted a baleful, soft glow of wet light off gun metal over behind the sentry's tree and fired at it. The guard let off a howl and dropped his gun.

Bill Haines, on one knee, fired straight down into the campfire. Men shouted and ran every which way. Jim Crawford, waiting for that sentry to show himself again, waited in vain. Evidently the guard had been disarmed by Given's shot. Old Cliffy danced from tree to tree in his pink-striped nightshirt and never got off a shot.

Far back, up near the horses but southward, two men yelled. That was enough for Bill who was worried about leaving their animals unguarded anyway. He sprang up and went running back the way they had come. Given sprang up and ran. Cliffy and Jim also fled back through the forest. Behind them men were unlimbering with six-guns and carbines well away from the campfire and someone with a furious, deep, and snarling voice was urging the others to rush whoever was out there.

Fortunately this did not fall on receptive ears, at least not immediately, for Given and Haines got astride, along with Jim and old Cliffy, and fled straight westward before there was any pursuit.

The gunfire continued, though. They could still hear it very plainly even after they were well beyond range.

CHAPTER
THIRTEEN

The pursuit was fierce and unrelenting. Given thought the cow thieves wouldn't push this accidental fight but evidently the knowledge that they were not alone in the night, confirmed twice now, gave O'Brien's gun hands a strong incentive to do their fighting when they couldn't do any trail driving — at night.

Bill Haines, riding twisted half around, kept Given apprised. He and Given were the last two to get clear. Cliffy and Jim, one on either side, were perhaps a hundred yards ahead.

"Had their damned horses saddled and ready," said Bill. "Otherwise, they'd never have been able to take after so quick."

Given heard and heeded but did not act really interested in *how* the pursuit had happened to boil out after them so quickly; he acted vastly more concerned with the lagging steps of his over-burdened horse. He gestured for old Cliffy to come closer. When the liveryman did, Given yelled to him to carry Haines for a while, and, when his horse began to tire, to pass Bill on across to Jim Crawford.

The perilous transfer was made in mid-gallop, no small feat for a man Haines's age who'd not too long before been battered senseless by a bucking horse, and, furthermore, it was made while all three horses and all four men were swinging in and out among big trees in the watery gloom of full darkness.

The moment Given's horse had only half its burden again, the beast seemed to pick up speed. But obviously, with their animals running on nothing stronger than stamina, this race couldn't last much longer, so Given swooped in next to Cliffy and asked where they'd rest. The old man brandished his carbine straight ahead.

"Up ahead in them low hills," he croaked.

O'Brien's men sighted them from time to time but the big trees kept them safely from the intermittent gunshots, then Jim dropped back beside Given and these two, in order to buy more time for Bill and Cliffy, swung wide, turned back, and whipped in behind two opposite trees. When the first outlaws charged headlong into sight, they opened on them with blasting six-guns. Someone's horse went down end over end, back there through the trees, and the men running close behind yelled and tried to lift their own racing mounts over the wreckage. Two were successful but the third man plowed right into the fallen horse and piled up amid high shouts of alarm and surprise.

Jim and Given emptied their weapons scattering O'Brien's rustlers left and right. These men fired back but with no great attention to accuracy because they were too occupied in getting clear of those two deadly guns on ahead.

Given jerked his head. He and Jim whirled and went plunging along in old Cliffy's wake, reloading as they rode, and leaving it up to their mounts to avoid running head on into trees.

This tactic worked better than Given had hoped it might. They found Cliffy and Haines just entering the hilly country on ahead, and from far back there was no sound or sign of O'Brien's reavers.

These low, gravelly hills, Cliffy told them when they slowed and finally halted atop a knoll to look backward and listen, had been the hunting grounds of Nez Percés many years earlier. There was no underbrush because the Indians always set fire to it in the fall. There weren't nearly as many trees out here, either, except down in the deeper swales, for the same reason — they, too, had been burned off.

Jim looked around. "I've been through here," he stated, "but I can't say I know the country."

Cliffy puffed out his chest. "You don't have to know it, Deputy, because I hunted and roamed these hills before you were born. You just leave it to me."

Bill Haines, reloading on the ground beside Cliffy's horse, said: "Yeah, we've done that a couple of times tonight an' look where it's brought us."

Cliffy sniffed. "At least I'm still ridin' a horse," he said. *"Humph!"*

"Humph yourself," growled Bill, slamming his .45 back into its holster, reloaded. "Take your cussed foot out of the stirrup and shut up."

Cliffy kicked loose and Haines mounted behind him again. They rode down off the swell into a gloomy small cañon where there was a creek. Here, three of them remained with the tired animals, while Given scouted

172

eastward on foot, listening for the pursuit. He heard it, but O'Brien's men were riding in a southerly way, which would carry them safely past. He returned and reported. Jim and Bill were of the opinion that they should go north so that the outlaws would not find them, on their way back to the herd. Cliffy, though, thought this would be a very good time to hit the outlaw camp.

"Why?" demanded Haines indignantly. "What crazy notion you got in mind now?"

Cliffy said very matter-of-factly: "You need a horse, don't you?"

Given and Jim exchanged a look. Haines was balefully staring at the liveryman. He eventually said grudgingly: "All right, you old devil. This once you've had a good idea. But don't let it go to your head. Given, what say?"

Ed got back astride, kicked loose a stirrup, and waited for Haines to get up behind him. He didn't say a word. None of them did until, a mile back down out of the rolling country, Jim wondered aloud if they shouldn't *all* take fresh mounts from the trail herd's remuda.

"Yes," agreed Given, "and drop down below the herd, if we can, turn it, and head it back north."

"We'll never be that lucky," stated Haines, and he was right. They found the remuda without much trouble because the roped-in horses whinnied at the scent of strange horses. The little cooking fire was burning low now. Until Given saw that he'd had no idea how much time had passed since their narrow escape. Haines was lucky. There was a saddled horse in the remuda. Given rigged out a fresh mount, working as swiftly and surely as his companions also worked, forked leather, and leaned down to toss aside the rope gate so that the other animals could also run free. They were riding away from the rope corral when Cliffy hissed for silence and raised one arm to point. Down the quiet night came the unmistakable clatter of mounted men loping toward them. Moments later they even heard grumpy voices. Given barked and Cliffy wheeled away, leading off southward. The racket they made was heard by those approaching horsemen and someone wailed out an agonized cry that carried to every man.

"They cut back. They hit our camp an' run off the horses. Come on, after 'em, an' this time *get 'em!*"

Bill Haines, atop the powerful black horse that had been saddled, probably belonging to the downed sentry, snarled a curse, turned, and fired point-blank toward that voice. A man squawked back there, indicating Bill's slug had come uncomfortably close. Someone else back there fired at the flash of Haines's gun, but the bullet hit a tree.

The advantage lay now with the men from Younger. They conserved their fresh animals, though, realizing that these would be the last horses they would get, on the run southward down the right flank of the herd.

Those thunderous scarlet flashes in the night had brought some of the Swallowtail cattle to their feet. The herd began to stir uneasily, but it was a big gather; over on the left flank the gunshots had probably not even been heard.

Given caught up with Cliffy and leaned down to yell. "Forget it! We can't turn the herd with O'Brien behind us. Head back into those low hills again."

Cliffy dutifully swerved westward, cutting in and out of trees until he had a fairly straight run, then he swung northward. Behind them, O'Brien's crew still sped along, still occasionally taking a shot. When Cliffy twice changed course, it seemed to confuse the rustlers for a time. Given heard them calling back and forth to one another. He and Jim Crawford repeated their earlier tactic of dropping back, taking stands behind trees, and waiting to break up the rush of pursuing armed men. But that rush did not materialize, or, if it did, it didn't occur until long after those two had abandoned their tactic and had raced to catch up with the others.

They got back into the low hills where Cliffy seemed to know his way even with inadequate light. He led them around and through a maze of swales seeming always to bear westward until he ultimately halted to blow his horse and twist backward to count noses.

"They'll be huntin'," he acknowledged of their pursuers, "but the day they outsmart me in these hills, it'll also be a frosty night in hell."

But Bill Haines went back to look and listen despite Cliffy's assertions. When he returned a half hour later, it was to state that this time O'Brien and his outlaws hadn't made the same mistake, but were now fanned out across a broad front and were moving at a slow, careful walk.

Cliffy snorted. "That's danged foolishness. Leave the horses down here in the trees an' I'll show you why."

Given and Jim Crawford dismounted without argument, but Haines bent a powerfully skeptical look upon the old man. "I don't have much faith in your tricks any more," he grumbled. "And I don't want to wind up afoot again, so I'll stay an' watch the horses."

Cliffy took Given and Jim with him, swung around a low hill near its base, kept gradually climbing upward until they were atop the hill, then angled along from ridge to ridge bearing back westward again. It was much too dark for them to see the oncoming outlaws, but that worked both ways, with one variant, they couldn't be seen, either, until the outlaws were upon them, and the variant was elemental: It was easier to skyline a mounted man than it was a dismounted one.

This was proved some ten minutes after Cliffy led them through a scrub-oak thicket and suddenly jerked to a halt, dropped to one knee, and pointed. Dead ahead, walking his horse and riding with a bared Winchester balanced across his lap, was a thick-shouldered, alert, mounted man. He was heading straight for the scrub-oak thicket. Given swung left and right; there would be other men on either side of this one somewhere. The question was — how close? He drew Cliffy and Jim to him, whispered briefly, then they broke up, crawled away on each side of Given, and almost at once were lost to sight. Given got down flat in the grass where even in daylight it would have been difficult to discern him.

The outlaw halted once to listen, then clucked at his horse. Given was on the man's left with the scrub-oak thicket behind him. He waited until the last possible moment; the outlaw was less than twenty feet away. Given got both hands hooked under his body, set his legs with both toes dug in, took a long breath, and waited a moment, then sprang. The horse did not see him at once. Neither did the outlaw. He had the man by the belt before the horse snorted and whirled toward Given, adding momentum to Given's lunge. The outlaw reached for his carbine but didn't quite make it because the horse reared, flinging the rider back hard against the cantle, across the startled horse's rump, to fall in a threshing heap onto the grass. The horse emitted a snort and bolted. He did an odd thing, though; he halted 100 feet away, spun, and looked back.

The outlaw was a big, powerful man, but things had happened too fast. In another place he might have been more than a match for Given. Now he wasn't. Still, even flat on his back with half the wind knocked out of him, he put up a savage fight.

Given saved himself by blocking a wild blow hurled at his head. He anticipated the outlaw's going for his gun and broke that up with a knee. He set himself so as to avoid being rolled upon, cocked a fist, and, when the cowboy jerked his head off the ground, he ran straight into those hard knuckles. It didn't cold-cock him but he seemed temporarily to lose his will and his co-ordination. He continued to struggle, but weakly.

177

Given drew his .45 and pushed it up within four inches of the range rider's forehead. The man froze, stopped moving altogether, and blinked into that solemn, eyeless steel socket. Given moved back, got to his feet, and gestured for his captive to do the same. The man got up and muttered something. Given told him to be quiet.

Cliffy came out of the eastward night, peered at the Swallowtail rider, grinned, stepped in, yanked away the prisoner's six-gun, picked up his carbine, and turned when Jim Crawford came up leading the cowboy's horse. Jim and O'Brien's man exchanged a steady look. Jim said: "Hello, Bob. Long way from home, aren't you?"

Bob didn't answer. He fell to pushing his shirt tail back into his trousers and glowering at Given. That hard fall hadn't fazed him nearly as much as Given's punch had.

Jim told Given this one was Bob Mather, one of the first hands Colin O'Brien had hired on after O'Brien had taken over as range boss of Swallowtail. Given had nothing to say; he merely gestured with the gun back toward Bill and the horses.

They walked along with their captive, Crawford leading his horse. When Haines saw them, he stepped out with his .45 up and ready. Cliffy hissed at him, so Bill came closer, squinting. "Be damned," he muttered. "You got one. I thought it was *them*. Hey, this here is Bob Mather."

Given, holstering his weapon, said dryly: "So Jim said. An old friend of O'Brien's."

178

"Yeah," persisted Haines. "He's an old friend of Colin's, but that's not the point. Bob was the other feller with O'Brien at the robbery of Charley's safe."

Cliffy jumped closely in and peered. "Are you sure?" he asked.

Haines moved up, caught the big cowboy by the shirt, and said: "Well, how about it, Bob?"

Mather glared and didn't open his lips. Haines's grip tightened. He handed Cliffy his gun and balled up his freed hand. Mather's glare didn't lessen any but he understood the imminent threat and growled: "All right, I was the other one. What you goin' to do about it?"

Bill stepped back, bleakly smiling. "I'm for drawin' and quarterin' you," he said. "But this here is a joint effort. We'll have to talk it over."

"Talk," growled Mather. "It ain't goin' to do you no good."

CHAPTER
FOURTEEN

In reply to a question from Jim Crawford, Bill said that Charley had named the two men with O'Brien out behind his store when he'd been pleading with Haines not to shoot him. The four of them looked over at Mather. He only shrugged. His temper seemed to be improving, though, because he half grinned at Jim Crawford, saying: "What a lousy deputy you make, Crawford. Colin said we had nothin' to worry about from you an' he sure was right."

Given ran this through his mind and had a wry comment to make about it. "I don't know, cowboy. The deputy's still free and armed . . . you're not. It's only a matter of time before O'Brien and the rest of his crew aren't, either."

Mather gave Given a disdaining look. "You think so, mister? Well, you go ahead and play out your little game an' we'll see who comes out on top."

"We aim to do exactly that, Mather, but there's one thing I'd like to know . . . where is the fourteen thousand dollars?"

Mather's disdaining expression deepened. "Wouldn't you like to know?" he growled.

Bill Haines breathed a violent oath and stepped forward. Given threw out an arm. "Mather, I'll count to five, then we'll go to work on you. But a smart man wouldn't push his luck. We'll get others like we got you. Someone'll talk. It might as well be you, unless, of course, you'd rather have a busted nose and only half your teeth."

Mather caved in. He didn't know Given but he obviously *did* know Bill Haines. "Colin's got it. It's in a belt around his middle. You'll have to kill him to get it, an' I don't figure the four of you'll even come close to doin' that."

Given turned to Crawford as Haines stepped back. "Tie him, Deputy. Tie his horse, too. Leave them both here. If we come through this, we'll come back for him. If we don't . . ." Given shrugged, and walked over to his horse.

Three of them mounted up and sat like stone, watching Deputy Crawford take care of Bob Mather. There was profanity and bitter protests, but these things only made Jim fit a gag into Mather's mouth made of the outlaw's own neckerchief. They rode away with Mather flopping back there and indignantly choking.

"Want to try that again?" Cliffy asked Given hopefully. "Shouldn't be too hard."

Given said, "We'll see," and led them atop the hill where he'd knocked Mather off his horse. Up there, the four of them sat listening to the night. Evidently O'Brien's crew had swept on by without noticing yet that one man was missing from the center of their dragnet.

Haines had a worthwhile suggestion. "Boys, they'll go back to camp eventually. They probably won't miss

Mather until they come together down there. Why not get down there ahead of them, set up an ambush, and just wait? The alternative is more of this Indian fightin' . . . ridin' and runnin' . . . and I don't mind admittin' I'm a mite tender where you fellers who're used to saddle leather got calluses."

Given looked at Jim. He nodded. Old Cliffy shrugged as though favorable, but also as though he thought this plan of Bill's a prosaic way to complete their nocturnal battle.

"Lead the way," Given said, dropping back to ride with Haines.

Cliffy and Jim rode ahead. Crawford still had Bob Mather's two weapons. He handed the Winchester to Given and kept the .45 in his waistband.

Bill suddenly looked eastward and said: "Hey, look yonder. It's gettin' light over along the horizon. Where'd the night go?"

It was, indeed, brightening against the far meeting of earth and sky, and to Given as well as to the others it did seem improbable that they'd been running and fighting the entire night.

Crawford had an astute observation to make. "Once dawn brightens things up, we'll be in a lousy position. Providing O'Brien catches us down his sights."

"Don't fret none about that," chirped old Cliffy. "I'll show you how to get this ambush set up."

Haines glowered at Cliffy's back and muttered: "He'll show us. He'll show us how *not* to set up a damned ambush. Except for him . . . and his danged white nightshirt . . . they'd never have known we were out here."

Given gave Haines a look. "I've had enough of that," he said, rode 100 yards, and changed the subject. "How far west is O'Brien going to ride before he gives up and comes back?"

Bill had a sobering thought about that. "I hope not too far. He's got my cash in his damned money belt."

They got back down where the scent of the herd was strong again. Animals were stirring, were coming up out of their beds, and beginning to amble around in search of graze or browse. There was a faint, soft lowing down across that big open place where the cattle were. Cattle, like men, showed new life at dawn.

Cliffy demonstrated one facet of his peculiar personality; he remembered every foot of the area down near the herd they had previously ridden over and led the others over near where the empty rope corral was and beyond it back into a little belt of shaggy old pines. He sat a moment, looking outward down toward the herd and behind it, up where that cooking fire had been.

"Catch 'em goin' an' comin' from here," he said smugly.

Given agreed and dismounted. So did Jim Crawford. Haines probably also agreed, although he didn't say he did. Still, Bill got down and propped his Winchester beside a tree while he looked for a good protected spot to tie his Swallowtail horse.

They got into position, checked their weapons, and settled for the wait. Bill said those bumps he'd received the evening before were just now catching up with him. "Getting stiffer'n a ramrod in the back and legs. I hope that damned horse swallows a pine cone and chokes to death," he stated.

Given made a smoke, lit it under his hat, settled with his shoulders against a tree trunk, and silently smoked. When Jim Crawford asked if he was sleepy, Given shook his head.

"Just thinking of a medium rare steak about two inches thick smothered in fried spuds and onions," he replied.

Haines groaned.

In the eastward distance a wolf raised its snout to the purple heavens and sang a mournful song of loneliness. Countless little overhead stars, visible through the unkempt matting of pine limbs, winked and faded and brightened. An owl swooped past on completely silent wings. Jim Crawford looked thoughtfully out where the cattle were beginning to drift.

"O'Brien's got to get back soon or his critters are going to drift and scatter. He'll realize that."

"Maybe," offered Cliffy, "he kept right on going. After all, he's had plenty of time to return."

"Don't even *think* a thing like that!" exclaimed Bill Haines. "Cliffy, he's got some of your money under his shirt, too, y'know."

"Yeah, I know, Bill. But with me money's not as important as it is with you."

"Yeah? Well, I'll tell you one thing, you old coot, a man can do a heap more with money than he can do without it."

184

Given removed his cigarette and lifted his head. "Shut up," he growled.

They slowly came erect and alert, straining to hear whatever it was Given might have picked up in the stirring pre-dawn coolness. For a while there was nothing, then it came out of the northward and southward gloom, men riding slowly, cautiously, back out to the west.

"Scattered wide this time," said Given. "Listen."

The men were scattered wide, but even Given had no idea exactly *how* wide. Evidently Colin had given the order to start the herd moving, but he'd been too wary to send all his riders down to do this. Given saw that northward rider up above where the fire had been. He kept hearing the southward cowboy but he never saw him. He slowly got upright to look and listen, a puzzled frown settled across his features. Something wasn't just right here. It wasn't simply that only two of the outlaws were coming back; it was something more than that. Given could feel it, could sense it, but he couldn't pin it down.

Over to the east the herd began to bawl and stir around, to mill and mix and amble in and out of the trees. Given concentrated on that for a moment before it struck him what was happening. He swung and barked at the others.

"Get into your saddles! Never mind the ambush! We've been out-maneuvered!"

The men jumped to obey but they asked quick, breathless questions, catching some of the contagion of Given's frantic haste. By the time he swung to ride

185

away, those distant eastward cattle were beginning to line out and bawl and bring all the rest of the animals along ahead of them.

"They got around over there," Given said, breaking clear of the trees and looking over his shoulder. "Got behind the cattle to the east and are setting them for a stampede straight toward us. O'Brien doesn't know *where* we are, but he knows which direction we'll be in, and with a herd that size, stampeding, they'll sweep a front two miles wide. Follow me and don't stop. No matter what happens, don't stop!"

The cattle were gathering momentum. That northward rider was no longer visible anywhere. The southward man couldn't be heard, either, because of the steadily increasing low rumble of cattle being pushed due westward.

Haines cried out: "If he can run us down, it's all that'll save his bacon!"

Given got clear of the last trees and lifted his animal into a lope. Where the trees thinned out, a stampede could be murderous. Four men and four horses could disappear under those thousands of hoofs and never leave a trace.

A man's clear, high shout came quivering through the watery light from somewhere north and east. In the echoing wake of that obvious signal, guns flashed orange and boomed out their terrifying thunder behind the herd. It sluggishly began to gather an irresistible momentum. Given watched as he raked his horse and sped along. He and the others were now running directly across the middle of that shaggy sea of blind-running, slobbering animals.

The guns popped and roared. Men yelled and hooted. These were small, insignificant sounds. The terrifying, dull roar of 4,000 charging cattle running wild soon drowned out everything else.

Bill Haines shot past Given. Old Cliffy came up even, with pre-dawn light showing his wreathed, seamed face; he wasn't smiling now. Jim Crawford swung up, also. He was riding a stocky little bay mule-nosed horse that had never been designed for high speed or sustained racing, but the horse was doing his best, either for the man atop him or because he sensed his peril.

They raced past trees and smelled the mustiness of death with the oncoming herd sweeping steadily closer. Occasionally a critter, blind with panic, struck a tree head-on. Other cattle piled up, creating a wild mound of threshing confusion. Other cattle split out around those heaps and raced straight ahead. It took nearly thirty minutes of hard riding before Given could see the upper or northward wing of the stampede, where the cattle were fewer and farther between. He kept riding until the last animals were behind, then put a congratulatory hand upon his mount's neck and drew back steadily to bring the excited horse down to an eventual halt. Around him the other three swerved and slowed and also eventually halted. Less than 100 yards behind them the farthest wing of the stampede rattled by with hoofs making the earth tremble and with

187

wicked, upcurving, wide horns clicking where they touched.

"Lord A'mighty," said Bill, badly shaken. "That was too close. Ed, if you hadn't suspected what was comin', we'd never have made it. It was so close I'm still shaking."

Given dismounted and walked his winded horse up and down. The others followed his example. In this manner they cooled out their horses and, also, settled their own raw nerves.

It took a long time for that herd to go past. Afterward, the air was so rank it choked them. Cliffy halted in his walking, looked westerly, and said: "He's done for, boys. That prisoner in the swale out there . . . he's done for. Them critters'll grind him to jelly."

Given halted, turned, and thought a moment, then resumed his walking back and forth, his expression solemn. He quite obviously agreed with Cliffy's assessment; they'd left Mather about a mile southward and a mile or a mile and a half westward — directly in the path of the stampede. They hadn't deliberately doomed him, of course, but that didn't alter the fact that, except for leaving him back there, he probably would have survived.

The last cattle were shambling past when Jim Crawford called softly and pointed. There were riders visible through the choking dust, still brandishing six-guns. They had neckerchiefs up over their faces and were loping along.

Given swung swiftly up over his leather and looked back. The others were doing the same. Bill Haines had his carbine in one hand, his reins in the other. He looked very business-like. Even old Cliffy, pink-striped nightshirt notwithstanding, appeared grim and ready. Given dropped his arm, jumped out his rested horse, and the others jumped out their mounts on both sides of him. The four of them headed straight down through the dust. Jim, the only one among them wearing a neckerchief, hoisted it up across his nose. None of the others noticed this and at the time Jim himself couldn't have attached any significance to his action except the usual one of a cowboy wishing to avoid having his nostrils and throat filled with choking dust.

The Swallowtail men were difficult to discern as they swung up and down the drag end of their stampede. They were too engrossed with their work to look around, either, which was fortunate for the men riding with Given, but when Bill Haines lowered his carbine and fired it one-handed, all that changed, for the Swallowtail men were using six-guns. The abrupt crash of a Winchester caught their attention instantly, bringing their eyes around so that they understood immediately they were being attacked by the very men they'd sought to run their herd over.

CHAPTER
FIFTEEN

For a moment of astonishment O'Brien's men looked and scarcely believed their eyes. They had obviously believed Given's party had been ground to mincemeat beneath all those hoofs. But that didn't last long because Haines and Cliffy howled and began shooting. The outlaws whipped around and fled. For the first time when both sides met, the men from Younger held the initiative.

Given pushed hard on the trail of the Swallowtail riders but he didn't shoot. Instead, he concentrated upon just locating and keeping the fleeing men in sight through the dust. It never occurred to Given, or to the others, that what they were chasing was less than half of O'Brien's crew. Through the dust it was impossible to make out more than one or two men at a time, but these same few riders could have been different men each time. At least Given and his companions, if they gave it much thought at all during the wild chase, must have believed this was so.

The herd was gone now, its earth-shaking rumble growing distant. O'Brien had lost some cattle. An inevitable happening in a stampede. Perhaps more to the point his scattered animals were far west of their regular southward trail to rail's end. O'Brien, the seasoned cowman, had demonstrated just how badly he wanted his attackers out of the way by ordering that stampede because to regather and line out the drive again would require at the very least one full day.

The ironic thing about it, Given thought, as he plunged ahead with Jim Crawford beside him, was that through all the fighting and maneuvering and running he hadn't once caught sight of Colin O'Brien. This thought was evidently uppermost in Jim's mind, too, because he suddenly turned and yelled over: "We got 'em now, Marshal! We got O'Brien now. Look through the dust yonder. They've gotten into those boulders and trees."

Given peered. Behind him, Cliffy and Bill Haines must have made this same observation because they let off taunting howls. Up ahead a carbine exploded. Given ducked instinctively, but none of them heard how close that slug had come, if it had been close at all. Cliffy was shouting and gesturing. They swerved and followed him over into a little spit of second-growth pine. There, they sprang down and grabbed at their carbines. It was hard to make out the place where those Swallowtail men had been forced to fort up, but it seemed to be perhaps 100 yards ahead where a collection of large rocks had somehow been tumbled together amid a scraggly growth of pines and firs.

The dust was lifting a little but not much. Visibility improved, although, as Cliffy said: " 'Tain't good enough to see *where* they are. We got to see them, too." He would have gone away westward except for the strong right arm of Bill Haines that closed fiercely down over his skinny shoulder.

"You stay right here an' never mind tryin' to flush 'em out of their lousy rocks. We'll get 'em out all together."

Cliffy writhed under that strong grip. "Leggo my shoulder, you dog-goned old money-grubbin' whiskey peddler, you!"

Haines let go, probably not because of Cliffy's importunings but because someone over in the trees and rocks fired and a bullet hit a tree four feet from Bill's head. He released Cliffy and dropped to one knee all in one smooth motion. He raised his carbine and let fly with an answering slug. They all clearly heard that bullet flatten viciously against rock.

Given and Jim Crawford stepped behind trees. Given said: "Cliffy, you and Bill take the horses back a ways and tie them out of harm's way. Then get back here."

Jim Crawford paused to take off his neckerchief and rub smarting eyes with it. "Damned dust," he growled. Given had a dry comment about that.

"Don't cuss it, Deputy, thank it. But for the dust we'd never have gotten this close. They can't see us any better than we can see them."

Two carbines opened on them from over amid the boulders. The men firing them seemed to believe they could smoke out Given and Jim by concentrated fire. They seemed to have plenty of ammunition, too, which Given and Crawford did not have, at least they hadn't enough to waste it like O'Brien's men were doing, so they flattened behind the trees, making no attempt to trade slug for slug, and weathered the storm in this fashion.

192

When Cliffy and Bill returned, they also had to get behind trees and stay out of sight. Bill called ahead, saying it sounded to him like they'd driven the whole band to cover. Given called back that all that racket up among the rocks was being made by just two riflemen. Haines said something in reply to Given's observation, but a bullet cutting an overhead limb and showering Haines with needles and pine cones turned his comment into blistering profanity. Nothing was as annoying as pine needles inside one's clothing. Haines risked a shot, and again they all heard lead flatten upon granite.

Daylight firmed up everywhere except in among the thickest stands of trees. There was still a mustard-like color to the atmosphere, though, left behind by O'Brien's stampede, and this more than anything else made marksmanship less a matter of skill and more a matter of pure chance.

Given studied the place up ahead where the Swallowtail rustlers were forted up. He called across to Jim that by now, wherever O'Brien and his other men were, they'd probably heard the shooting. Jim said he thought there had to be more than two men over there. Given agreed there might be three, but no more than that. There was a little lull during this exchange, then a man sang out from over in the rocks, and Given as well as his companions held their fire.

"Hey, Deputy!" the Swallowtail man sang out. "Hey, Crawford, can you hear me?"

"I can hear you."

"Well, listen, Crawford, you ain't got a chance. The rest of our bunch's creepin' in behind you right this minute. Play this smart, Crawford. Put down your gun . . . you an' those fellers with you . . . get astride an' head back for Younger. We got nothin' particular against you, so don't make us salt you down."

Jim looked across where Given was slowly dropping to one knee behind his tree, slowly raising his Winchester and taking a vice grip with the barrel in the crotch formed by thumb and forefinger tightly against the tree trunk. Jim swung his head, searching for whatever Given had evidently seen and was aiming at.

Given said sharply: "Talk, Deputy. He's stallin'. Keep talking."

Jim cleared his throat. "Who are you?" he asked. "How'd you ever let Colin talk you into anything like this? You can't get this herd sold. I've got enough men here with me . . ."

"Cut it out, Crawford," scoffed the hidden range rider. "There are four of you. One of 'em is Haines from the saloon in town, another's that old cuss from the livery barn. Then there's another feller an' you. Crawford, we got seven men. Them's bad odds, Deputy. Listen, we don't want to kill the lot of you. All we want —"

Given fired, a man jumped high into the air southwestward where he'd been stealthily crawling away from the protective boulders, let off a high scream, and collapsed, falling against a little pine tree like a broken doll, sliding down it, and crumpling over onto his side.

194

For a horrified second there wasn't a sound. None of the staring men had any doubt at all but that Given had killed the rustler.

The man over in the rocks who had been talking roared a wild string of oaths at Jim Crawford and snapped off two shots. Cliffy, evidently ready and waiting, fired straight at the dirty little puffs of smoke and must have come uncomfortably close because the man in the rocks did not fire again for a moment, and next time he'd gotten into a new position.

Bill Haines took advantage of a lull to call out: "Hey, you cow thief over in those rocks . . . how many men did you say O'Brien had?"

A different voice answered Bill, a gruffer, fiercer-sounding voice: "Six. But don't crow yet, barkeep. I'm waitin' for one good shot to exact payment for what you fellers just done."

"Five," croaked old Cliffy. "Bob Mather's dead, too." Cliffy seemed to wait, expecting derision or disbelief. When it didn't come, he said: "All we need's to pepper one more of you scum an' the odds'll be even. *Then* we'll see which side of your mouths you boys talk out of."

Once more the men in the rocks emptied their carbines as they'd done before, spraying lead back and forth and levering their weapons as fast as they could. Given thought they either were fools or had more Winchester ammunition in their pockets than range riders usually carried. It also struck him that the men were undoubtedly hoping their sustained gunfire would bring relief. It was this relief that troubled Given.

195

Undoubtedly O'Brien would hear this fight even if he was off to the west, turning back his exhausted cattle. Sooner or later he couldn't help but hear it. When that happened, he and his companions would be in trouble.

Given twisted to look around. Bill and Cliffy, to his right and left but also behind him, looked back and signalled that they were unhurt. It didn't seem to dawn on either of them that Given wasn't looking at them, that he was probing their back trail for sign of Colin O'Brien with the balance of his tough Swallowtail riders.

Jim Crawford fired, drawing Given's attention forward again. Over in the rocks an exposed leg was swiftly sucked back. Crawford's slug had been very close. The owner of that leg fired back spitefully; he couldn't see Crawford but he knew which tree Jim was behind. From time to time, probably just to make sure Crawford wouldn't repeat that near miss, the outlaw drove a slug into Jim's tree.

Given relieved this pressure when he drove two bullets at an angle into the rocks where the Swallowtail man was entrenched. Both slugs ricocheted and drove the range rider farther back into the rearward trees.

Jim looked over and smiled. Bill Haines, farther back, said something, but a savage little exchange drowned him out and involved him in another series of fierce bullet trades. When this latest exchange petered out, Bill called out again.

"Hey, up there! Cliffy's gone!"

Given whirled. So did Jim Crawford. Bill Haines pointed with his carbine toward the liveryman's tree, made a big jump, got over behind Cliffy's tree, and said: "See, he's not here."

"Which way do his tracks go?" Given asked sharply.

Haines was a moment answering that. "East. They go east over toward where the trees are thicker, Marshal, but I can't make out anything more than that. What should we do?"

"Nothing," growled Given. "Bill, don't try anything. We can't afford to lose another man hunting for him. Stay where you are."

"The damned old fossil," growled Haines. "I *knew* he'd do something goofy. I just *knew* it!"

"Watch where you fire from now on. I think we all know what he's up to. Trying to get around behind those two boys in the rocks. Be damned sure from now on before you squeeze a trigger."

For a space of perhaps three minutes the silence settled in, deep and menacing. It must have dragged at the raw nerves of O'Brien's forted-up cowboys as much as it also rubbed the raw nerves of the men from Younger. One of the rustlers cried out again.

"Crawford! Hey, Crawford!"

Jim looked over at Given. For a moment or two Given listened to that yelling man, then he shook his head. Jim understood. He kept silent.

"Hey, Crawford, dammit all, answer up!"

Haines hissed and Given turned and threw him a dark look. Bill subsided. The man in the rocks called out several more times before he eventually ceased. The stillness dragged out to its absolute limit. A gunshot erupted over in the rocks. Given signaled for neither

Crawford nor Haines to reply in kind. Another gunshot erupted, this one farther eastward but also in among the rocks. Given gave the same signal again.

For a while longer the stand-off went on. A man's muttering voice came distantly down to the place where Given stood. He tried to make out words but couldn't. He was much too far away. All the same, he surmised that O'Brien's two surviving cowboys were coming together in their hide-out to talk over this unprecedented silence. Given could imagine their dilemma. They would wish with all their hearts that the deputy and his friends had departed, but they wouldn't be so hopeful that they'd expose themselves.

Given looked at Crawford and Haines and winked. They both winked back. They understood what Given was doing: trying to give old Cliffy his chance.

"Come on, Deputy," that snarling, bitter-voiced man over in the rocks sang out. "We know you're still there. You're playin' a kid's game an' we ain't kids. Come on . . . speak up. We're ready to make a deal with you."

Crawford looked over and raised his brows. Given shook his head again. The sun was beginning to burn downward from half up its initial climb. The morning was advancing.

"Deputy. We'll walk out o' here, providin' you keep them men with you from pottin' us," the gruff man said loudly. "You ready to accept that? We'll come out without our guns. All right?"

Crawford and Haines looked at Given and once more got the same head wag. Bill screwed up his face into a grimace of mixed doubt and anxiety. Given ignored it.

"Deputy! Dammit all, man, speak out. We're surrenderin'. Show yourself so's we'll know which way to walk out o' here."

Now Given's expression toward Crawford and Haines was ironic. The other two understood. That man up in the rocks still wanted a life for a life. He meant to kill Jim Crawford through a ruse.

Far back behind Given's tree someone roared out into the tense hush and instantly Crawford and Haines spun round. Bill blurted out a name. "O'Brien!"

Given sagged against his tree. It had been very close, very close. He'd almost played cat-and-mouse this time and won, but O'Brien was coming up now with the balance of his men. The two in the rocks would have also heard him bellow, so now everything was changed.

CHAPTER
SIXTEEN

Given signalled for Haines and Crawford to follow him
and started eastward, but the three of them hadn't gone
more than fifty feet when a gun exploded southward
over behind the trees and rocks where O'Brien's men
still lay. At once someone let off a big howl that
culminated when two more guns opened up, but now
firing southward instead of northward.

Bill Haines said: "Cliffy!"

Given and Crawford turned as the bar owner started
ahead. Jim caught Haines and pushed him against a
tree. Bill snarled at the lawman. "You idiot, they'll skin
him alive with no one down there to help him. Let go!"

Given broke in, saying: "Not that direction, Bill.
Follow me." The two of them ran on eastward, but
Haines kept looking back, his face contorted. Those
guns traded shots again, silence ensued, and then more
shots were fired. Bill ran up to Given and protested.

"They're goin' to murder that old goat, out there all
by himself, Ed."

Given shook his head and turned to speak.
Northward men's yells rose and echoed through the
trees as Colin O'Brien and the balance of his
Swallowtail riders raced up.

Given kept running until the three of them were
away from being flanked by O'Brien, then turned

southward and hastened along in that direction. Until he did that, it didn't seem to dawn on Haines what Given was doing — trying hard to join Cliffy in flanking the men in the rocks.

Where they halted finally, for Given to get his bearings, Jim Crawford said: "Hell, they'll have our horses by now." Jim sounded more disgusted than hopeless.

"We'll get 'em back with interest," growled Bill, as Given grunted at them and started slowly inward toward a westerly juncture with Cliffy down behind that bed of boulders somewhere.

"He'd have pulled it off this time," Given said, "if O'Brien hadn't come up. The old cuss has his share of grit."

For once Haines had no derogatory remark to make. All the same he looked like he'd enjoy taking his belt to Cliffy.

The gunfire was intermittent now. Obviously Colin O'Brien wasn't sure who was who over in those trees and rocks. He wasn't joining the fight yet, which gave Given more time.

They came through a sage thicket into a bosque of stunted oaks, passed beyond this to a light stand of pines, and halted where two old junipers stood side-by-side, evidently growing out of the same root stock. From this place they had a very good view of the land ahead. They didn't see Cliffy in his nightshirt but they saw gray smoke arise when someone over behind a dead fir tree fired forward into the rocks.

Instantly two shots came back. Both struck the old dead fir tree. Haines grimaced. "They know where he is."

Given raised his carbine. "Well," he said calmly, "let's give him a chance to change that." Given drove a slug straight over into the rocks. He had a good view of where they were hidden, but still none of them could see the Swallowtail men.

From back up north Colin O'Brien sang out. His men in the rocks, however, were too occupied now with all four of their original attackers to answer. They threw lead out where Given had fired from, got back some angry shots from Bill and Jim, and were driven by this murderous crossfire deeper into cover.

Cliffy hooted and shot from a different position. Each time he fired now, he gave that same high howl of glee. He understood what had happened and kept moving from tree to tree until he was less than 100 feet from the trees shielding his friends. Once he poked his tousled white thatch out and made a gobbling sound like a wild turkey. Bill Haines, in the act of aiming, lifted his head, squinted around, and vigorously shook his fist at the old man.

O'Brien was getting closer to the rocks. He had now evidently figured out which were his men and which were his enemies. He called out and got back an immediate, desperate-sounding reply from in the rocks. Given also turned, as did Haines and Crawford, toward this new menace. Only old Cliffy Hart remained as obdurately set on flushing those two desperate men out of the boulders as before.

Given sighted someone whipping from tree to tree toward the besieged men. He fired, missed, levered up, and fired again. This shot was close enough to drive that flitting shadow to cover; he did not charge ahead again, either.

Colin O'Brien's rumbling voice commanded the men in the rocks to keep down and leave Crawford to him. This brought a hard comment from Bill, who was hoping to sight the Swallowtail range boss.

"We're waiting!" he shouted to O'Brien. "Colin, we're waiting, so come on and let's get this over with."

O'Brien's answer came right back. "I'm comin', Haines . . . damn you. I'm comin'."

It got very quiet again. Given dropped to one knee, half twisted to spear the rearward woods with a rummaging glance, and looked back at the others. They had followed his example and were also down on their knees. The stalking and the waiting went on. Meanwhile, those two men in the rocks called out every once in a while to direct O'Brien and his companions. They knew where Given and Crawford and Haines were. Cliffy shut up those two briefly by peppering their hiding place, but Given gestured for Cliffy to desist and save his bullets.

The sun brightly shone. Distantly plaintive bawls of cattle rolled in with the changing breezes. It was getting hot even in the shade. There was a powerful scent of pine sap. The men from town hadn't had a drink of water since the night before and hadn't had a bite of anything to eat since long before that. Moreover, they'd been moving fast and spending energy recklessly for a

203

long time. The result of all this was twofold. They became drowsy in the heat and silence even when at the same time they were raw-nerved and impatient to finish their battle. Only old Cliffy Hart, dehydrated and thin as a rail, seemed not to run out of enthusiasm. When Given, swinging to see where Cliffy was, looked, the old man was gone. Given's eyes flashed but he said nothing; he only pointed. Jim and Haines also saw that tree where Cliffy had been. Jim showed nothing but resignation. Haines's face got red as a beet. If it hadn't been a matter of life and death that he remain strictly silent now, he would have turned the air blue. As it was, he faced around and dropped prone, pushed his carbine ahead, and concentrated his full fury ahead, where O'Brien and his range riders would probably appear.

The wait was long. Crawford dug at both eyes with balled fists. Given followed Bill's example and lay flat, but from time to time he shook his head as though to fight off an increasing lassitude.

Bill fired, levered frantically, and fired again. A tall cowboy stepped from behind a tree, stared in Bill's direction, looking astonished, dropped his carbine, took two steps forward, and fell forward on his face as stiff in the legs as though he'd been made of steel.

Guns exploded on both sides of where that man had been. Gray smoke rose up in small, gray puffs. Bullets raked blindly through the trees overhead as Colin and his riders tried to locate Haines, the one who had killed that scouting cowboy. Given yelled for them to roll after each shot and set the example. He'd fire, roll, lever up, and fire again. He did that six times, then stopped, raised up, and hurled his empty Winchester straight over into a chaparral thicket. A startled outlaw sprang up, swinging his own carbine by the stock, evidently thinking himself under personal attack. Given shot at this man with his handgun but missed. Jim didn't miss. He drove a slug straight into the thicket from a stiff arm rest and the cowboy bellowed in pain, turned, and jumped over behind a tree. He didn't stay there, but jumped back and forth behind other trees, retreating all the time.

"The odds are getting better!" exclaimed Haines, and raised up to fire. A bullet came out of nowhere, struck the barrel of Bill's gun, traveled down to the stock, and violently knocked the gun ten feet away, breaking the wood into kindling. Bill flopped over onto his side, dazed and bleeding at the cheek where a sliver had gouged him.

Given saw the whole thing. He started to roll over toward Haines, but Jim Crawford sprang up, ran over, grabbed Haines, and dragged him back. Three six-guns opened up. Given drove lead toward them both, spoiling the aim of Colin's men.

Jim got Haines behind a tree and Given slackened off his fire when he heard Bill's bull-bass, angry voice indignantly ordering Crawford to let go of his shirt. Bill would be all right.

Over to the south again, facing into the field of rocks, Cliffy's yells and gunshots erupted. A man let off a high-pitched wail of anguish. Cliffy had finally gotten one of those snipers in the rocks. He howled like an

Indian over this small triumph and engaged the surviving rustler in a savage pistol duel, screeching like a maniac all the while.

Jim crawled over to Given and reported that he'd wrapped his neckerchief around Bill's face to stop the bleeding and had left his Winchester with Haines. Then the pair of them waited for that wild fight between Cliffy and the man in the rocks to end. Evidently O'Brien also was waiting for the same thing because now there was no more firing from the eastern woods.

Cliffy's shouting abruptly halted. So did the gunfire. Given craned around. It had sounded to him as though old Cliffy had stopped a bullet in mid-cry. Crawford started to turn. Given halted him with an outflung arm. "Stay here," he ordered. "If we split up now, we're not going to get out of this."

"But I think he's hit," Crawford protested.

"Stay here, anyway!" exclaimed Given, facing forward again. "They're up to something. It's too quiet."

There wasn't a sound from the yonder trees where O'Brien had been. It was the same kind of a silence that had preceded Given's original stalk toward the boulder heap. He jerked his head at Jim. They crawled back where Haines was sitting, his face and shoulders splattered with scarlet, his bandage soggy with blood. He looked like he was nearly dead except in the eyes. Bill was furious. He gripped Jim's carbine with white-knuckled hands and glared, even at Given.

"Where are they?" he demanded in a hoarse whisper. "I want another one. Show me that whelp that busted my carbine, damn his lights!"

206

"Stalking us, I think," said Given. "Crawl back a ways so we can keep plenty of ground between us and them. Come on."

Bill looked over at the rock pile. "Where's that consarned old coot?" he demanded.

Neither Jim nor Given answered him. They both started belly-crawling westward. They had to cross in front of the rock pile but this was the only way. Even if that surviving rustler was still holed up in there, they still had to risk it. Given took the lead and kept it. He alternately watched the rocks and their back trail. When he thought he spied movement, once, he rolled behind a log and motioned the others to do the same. No shots came though, so they crawled on again.

The sun hit down through the limbs and heat began rolling up. Given led them safely past the boulders without drawing a shot, tunneled through a chaparral thicket, and sat up inside it. Bill and Jim got in there with him. The chaparral was no protection at all against bullets, but it was more than adequate to hide them from peering eyes. Haines removed the neckerchief, wrung it out, and retied it. "I'm goin' to have a bad scar right across my cheek from this," he muttered.

Crawford looked at him. "At least it's a scar from a fight," he whispered, "instead of you gettin' hit in the face with a beer glass in your saloon."

Haines bent a caustic look upon the deputy. "Yeah, but there's a considerable difference, my young friend," he growled. "No one ever dies of gettin' hit by beer glasses."

Given silenced them and took off his hat, pushed his face deeply into the spiny limbs, and was as still as stone for a full minute before he gently eased back again.

"What'd you see?" Bill asked.

"Two of them. They're sneaking around into the rocks."

"Well, there's more'n just two left," Haines muttered. "So that means two are goin' to try an' rout us from the left and maybe two from the right."

"Not if they don't know where we are," put in Jim, and had his mouth open to say something else when a wild burst of gunfire erupted off to the north. A man's startled squawk burst out. Another man called someone by name. If there was an answer, it got drowned out by more firing. From southward among the rocks O'Brien's unmistakable voice shouted a quick, breathless question. There was no answer but the men crouching stiffly in their thicket heard spurred boots furiously running back toward the eastward trees again.

The firing ceased as abruptly as it had begun. Jim and Bill exchanged a bewildered glance. Given shoved his face into the bushes again, drew back, and picked up his hat without a word, crushed it on his head, and sat down, wagging his head from side to side. As he raised his face, he said: "Make way, company's coming."

Cliffy came noiselessly slithering into the thicket, his nightshirt torn and soiled, his mop of white hair standing on end. He wiggled on in, sat up, and said quietly: "Any of you boys spare an old man some shells for a Forty-Five? I done shot out my last loads when I stumbled onto them varmints out there."

Bill opened his mouth and glared. He closed it without saying a word. He fished around among the loops of his belt, drew forth six bullets, and passed them over.

"We thought they'd gotten you," said Crawford.

The old man began reloading his six-gun. "Nope. I wanted 'em to think that. Then I snuck around 'em and run northward a ways and —"

"Why northward?" blurted Haines. "You lost your reason? The fighting's right down here."

Cliffy looked up with a little, cherubic grin. "I know that, Bill, I know that. But first I had to set 'em afoot, didn't I? I told you boys last evenin' with half a chance I could do it, didn't I? Well, I had to keep my word."

Given said: "Cliffy, you turned their horses loose?"

"Yup," stated the old man. "Cut every *cincha* and set 'em loose. Let's see what Mister O'Brien can do about *that!*"

CHAPTER
SEVENTEEN

Given was almost afraid to ask but he asked anyway: "Cliffy, what about *our* horses?"

"Took 'em westward a ways and re-hid 'em. *We'll* ride back, but *they* won't."

Over in the rocks a man's fluting call sounded. He seemed to be facing eastward when he sang out. For a moment there was no reply, but eventually one came and whoever made it sounded cautious. Cliffy chuckled.

"They're bein' real careful now, those two I routed. You should've seen the looks on their faces when I jumped out at 'em."

"I can imagine," murmured Given dryly, thinking of the sight old Cliffy undoubtedly presented to anyone not expecting a wild-eyed, tousle-headed old scarecrow attired in a pink-striped nightshirt with a blazing gun in his hand.

The men calling back and forth got closer. The ones from through the eastward trees were making for the rock pile. Given and the others, in their place of concealment, could follow the course of O'Brien's men by the noises.

Bill Haines said that by his count there could not now be more than four men with Colin O'Brien, including the range boss himself, and at least one of those men had to be wounded. He also said he thought it was time they went on the offensive. Given agreed with this but sat on for a while longer in the chaparral, waiting for those rustlers to come together. He was thinking, and, after the outlaws ceased their noise, Given checked his six-gun's loads and started crawling northward out of their thicket. The others followed and said nothing until they were well away, then Jim got up beside the ex-lawman and wanted to know what Given had in mind.

"Back there," explained Given, "we had to wait until they were together to make certain it was safe for us to leave. But now they're going to guess that we're between them and the horses."

"*Ahhh*," sighed Haines, "I understand. They'll make a rush to reach their animals before we get to them." Haines bleakly smiled. "They don't know they don't have any horses. Let's go."

They went on, running a little now from time to time when there was adequate cover to make this feasible. Cliffy hissed at Given after a while and gestured westward. They all halted. Cliffy said they'd better get over closer to where their own animals were, otherwise O'Brien might stumble onto them and reverse the thing, leaving the men from Younger on foot.

Given agreed and turned, but now Cliffy took the lead. He rushed along with his nightshirt flapping until they came to a clump of mixed trees. There, patiently drowsing, were their saddled Swallowtail horses. Haines heaved a noisy sigh of relief.

"Cliffy, if you were a hundred years younger an' a female, I could kiss you," he gloated.

Cliffy sniffed and turned away, embarrassed. Given told Haines to stay with the horses, to get astride one and keep the reins to the others in his hand. He then sent Cliffy off on one side, Jim Crawford on the other side, and took the center position himself. When he signaled, Haines got aboard, scooped up the reins, and walked their animals farther back westward. Jim and Cliffy waved back at Given and those three began a slow, cautious advance eastward, which would put them in a flanking position when O'Brien came.

The heat was strong now, even where shade lay. This had an adverse effect for the Swallowtail men, too; it made the brush underfoot dry and crackly. Even Indians wearing moccasins couldn't have crossed through here without making noise. Men with spurs on their heavy boots didn't have a chance of concealing their approach, particularly as O'Brien and his men now were coming in an anxious hurry hoping to save their animals.

Cliffy saw them first, or at least heard them first. He fired. Given and Jim exchanged a look, both obviously wishing the old man hadn't done that. At once O'Brien's men faded back and returned Cliffy's shot. Bullets spattered through the trees, mostly high and searching.

Given caught Cliffy's eye and motioned for him to hold his fire. For a moment the rustlers kept it up, then they, too, ceased firing. Given called out to them.

"O'Brien, you're afoot! Give it up!"

Given ducked and rolled, expecting a gunshot by way of an answer. It proved an unnecessary precaution. No shot came. For a moment there wasn't a sound anywhere. Finally, though, the range boss called back to Given.

"Is that you, Jim?"

Crawford answered: "No. That's an ex-deputy U.S. marshal, Colin. The same feller who made your two men fight Cuff's boys up in town. He's been leadin' this show. I haven't. His name's Given. Edward Given."

There was another brief interlude of silence before O'Brien sang out again: "Hey, Given . . . or whatever your name is . . . how'd you like to be rich?"

Given's reply was short. "At my age, O'Brien, that's not important any more. You had enough?"

"No. But you'll have had enough if you don't back off."

"Oh," said Given dryly, "you figure to drive that herd to rail's end on foot?"

"Listen, Given, let's cut this out. You let us get our horses and we'll cut you a big slice of the pie."

"I told you, O'Brien, I'm not interested. Now let *me* tell you something. You've got at least one wounded man. The rest of you are going to get hurt just as bad and maybe worse, so throw in the towel."

"Go to . . ."

"Wait a minute, O'Brien. Think a little. You can't get away on foot. You've lost the herd because you can't drive it without mounts, and we're still as strong as ever. The worst you'll get is maybe ten years in prison.

213

Maybe less. Even ten years is better than dying, isn't it?"

Jim Crawford let off a sharp cry and fired. Given rolled immediately and none too soon. Evidently, while he'd been trying to reason with O'Brien, the rustlers had been fanning out to close in. One of them had inadvertently been spotted by Crawford, but O'Brien himself, with a roar of rage, had blasted away in the direction of Given's voice. It had been very close, too. Dust and bark showered the ex-lawman as he rolled away.

Cliffy screeched indignantly and drove two shots toward the muzzle blast of a man directly opposite him. It was this howl that diverted the attention of the attackers and permitted Given to scramble in behind a punky old deadfall. There, he raised up and fired three times, fast. There was nothing to aim at but there didn't have to be; he only wished to drive their attackers back into the trees again and in this he succeeded.

For a moment the fight raged, then gunfire dwindled again. This time, though, no one spoke. O'Brien was clearly dedicating himself now to the complete eradication of his enemies. Given lay low, reloading. He finished with that little chore, twisted anxiously to peer backward for a sighting of Haines and their horses, saw nothing, and turned back, looking relieved. Haines was a hot-tempered man. He'd proved that to everyone's satisfaction in the last twenty-four hours, but all the same Given didn't want him to leave the horses and rush back to help. The horses were more important to both sides now than the Swallowtail herd or even that $14,000 inside Colin O'Brien's shirt.

Jim fired once, off on Given's left, and was silent. Cliffy, too, was quiet for a change. Given raked the shadowy places in front of his deadfall, saw nothing, and began to worry. He drew away from the shielding old downed tree and cautiously worked his way over to join Cliffy. But when he got where Cliffy had been and should have still been, no one was there. Given looked and sighed and shook his head. Old Cliffy was going to get killed yet, playing Indian.

A loud wolf bark sounded over through the trees behind where O'Brien's men were. Given swore under his breath. He had no idea how Cliffy had gotten around there so fast but he recognized that simulated bark as belonging to the old man. Evidently O'Brien also knew an enemy had made that sound for a gun abruptly opened up, firing eastward. When another .45 opened up in the same direction, Given briefly held his breath.

Jim Crawford, seeking to divert some of this fire, yelled O'Brien's name and let drive with two quick shots. Given joined in by also firing, but holding low to the ground when he did for fear of possibly nicking old Cliffy who was also in the direction he shot.

O'Brien, caught between two fires, fought desperately. If he stopped to reload, Given couldn't discern when he did it. Also, Given counted four guns in the yonder trees, not the three he'd thought would be over there. Apparently that injured rustler hadn't been put out of action, after all.

Something on his left caught Given's attention. He spun half around. Jim Crawford was crawling swiftly toward him on all fours. Jim had to be motivated by some compelling reason to take this chance. Given held his fire, eased around behind a giant pine, and waited. Jim came up, breathing noisily, and squeezed into cover.

"Three horses," he stated, pointing over in the direction he'd crawled from. "I saw 'em and fired thinkin' it was men. They've got saddles on."

Given frowned. They couldn't be *their* horses. Haines had gone west. He groaned. "If Bill's returned, I'll shoot him," he said.

But Jim shook his head. "Not ours, Marshal. I didn't recognize any of them. I tried scattering them with gunfire but hell they're *tied*. They yanked back and jumped around but couldn't break loose."

"Show me," Given said, beginning to crawl back the way Jim had just come. The pair of them made haste but were also careful. Over through the trees Cliffy was still occasionally letting off one of his hair-raising yells and firing. O'Brien was answering those shots, which was a godsend for Given and Jim Crawford. Even when they got down to where Jim halted and pointed toward several partially hidden saddled animals, Cliffy was still firing and yelling.

A tall man suddenly emerged through the forest, running headlong. It was one of O'Brien's riders and he'd obviously also seen those horses.

Jim grunted. "That one's had enough." He started to jump up to rush the outlaw, but Given, down on one knee, stopped him. "It could be a trick. Use your gun."

216

Both of them raised their pistols. The rustler had one horse untied. He swung the animal crossways so that its body shielded his own body. Jim swore and waited. So did Given. Now they had to let the rustler step up over leather before they could pick him off. The man jammed a boot into a stirrup and sprang high. The saddle turned. Man and leather crashed together to the ground. The horse set back in earnest at this unprecedented event, snapped his reins loose, stumbled over the man who was threshing helplessly under the saddle, and fled wildly northward through the trees.

The rustler, evidently grazed by a foreleg, a shod hoof or a knee, raised up dazedly and flopped back, still with the saddle across his body. Given jumped with a grunt and raced ahead. Crawford also started ahead, but at the last moment he halted, raised his gun, and searched the surrounding cover for any enemy who might have seen Given.

O'Brien's rider was recovering from his shock when Given came up and dived straight at the cowboy. Given clubbed an overhand blow with his six-gun which the cowboy saw descending and rolled frantically to save himself. He made it, but the pile of leather still constricted his movements. He tried to lunge upward and regain his feet but Given didn't give him the chance. He rolled over, got up onto one knee, and pushed his cocked .45 into the rustler's face. All the frantic threshing ceased as the rustler stared into that black hole.

Given got up, stepped over beside a tree, and motioned the rustler to disengage himself and stand up.

217

The man obeyed, still acting slightly loggy. He glowered and flexed his right hand, but there was no longer any six-gun in his hip holster; it had evidently fallen out during his recent travails.

Given gestured with the gun in Jim Crawford's direction. The two of them were moving off when old Cliffy's high, cackling laughter rang boomingly through the forest. The outlaw winced at that sound. Even Given turned to look back. Old Cliffy was coming through the shadows using his Winchester to brush aside low hanging limbs.

Crawford poked a gun into their prisoner's side and backed him against a tree. Cliffy came up, profusely sweating and more disheveled than ever, carrying two canteens slung across his shoulders. He smiled broadly at the sullen captive, unslung the canteens, and handed one each to Jim and Given. Then he said: "Got to figurin', while I was whippin' around behind 'em, that since I knew about where their danged critters were with their busted *cinchas*, I'd set up a little trap. And danged if it didn't catch a skunk, at that."

Jim and Given exchanged a look. Given smiled. It was the first time Crawford had ever seen the ex-lawman smile. Jim smiled back, drank deeply from the canteen, handed the thing back to Cliffy, and said he thought they ought to tie up their captive. At once old Cliffy stepped in to take care of that. He punched the much larger, much younger man in the stomach with his cocked carbine.

"Sit down, friend," he chortled. "This won't hurt. In fact, the way I got this figured, I'm doin' you a big favor. You're likely to live through all this. O'Brien ain't goin' to, an' I got a feelin' them other two fellers with him might not. *Sit down!*"

Over through the brush O'Brien called out again. This time he addressed himself to Given. "Hey, Marshal. You ready to quit now?"

Cliffy poked his sitting prisoner again. "Yell out an' tell him you're a prisoner an' let's see what reaction that gets." Cliffy grinned so hard it seemed his face would crack.

CHAPTER
EIGHTEEN

"Hey, Colin! This here is Freitas. Bill Freitas. They got me an' they ain't goin' to quit. Don't go near them damned horses that're tied up northward in the trees. It's a trap."

Cliffy threw back his head and made one of his Indian yells. Jim scowled over at him. The four of them were safely behind a huge old fir tree but even so Crawford didn't like the idea of Cliffy's drawing O'Brien's wrathful gunfire in their direction.

However, no gunfire came.

Given said: "Cliffy, you and Jim keep watch. I want to talk to Mister Freitas here." As the pair of friends moved off, Given knelt to finish the tying job old Cliffy had begun. He spoke conversationally as he did this, and, if their prisoner's sullen expression didn't lessen much, at least his eyes showed interest in Ed Given.

"How much did O'Brien promise you boys for helping him, Freitas?"

"A thousand apiece . . . after we peddled the herd. And a bonus of another thousand if there was a fight an' we stood by him."

Given looked up. "Two thousand apiece? Hell, man, that herd alone will bring more than enough to make each of you independent for life."

Freitas made a crooked smile. "Well, now, mister," he drawled. "We wasn't at rail's end, either, you know." Freitas's dark eyes were hard and merciless in their steady stare at Given. Plainly he and the other men with O'Brien had talked among themselves. Given nodded. O'Brien was a loser, one way or another he was a loser, and the ironic part of it was he had no inkling yet that he was.

"I see," murmured Given. "You boys sort of figured you were entitled to a little more."

"A *lot* more, mister."

Given finished with the tying, examined his handiwork, was satisfied with it, and stood up. "Tell me, Freitas, how can we get those men with O'Brien to stop fighting us?"

"You can't!" exclaimed the burly captive. "But even if you could, they'd never let you take Colin because they know what's in his money belt. Fourteen thousand dollars."

Given nodded, his expression turning thoughtfully wry. O'Brien didn't stand a chance. Given walked over where Cliffy was, made certain the old man hadn't pulled one of his disappearing tricks again, turned, and waved for Jim Crawford to join them. The moment Jim came up, Given related all that Freitas had said. Jim looked pained but not surprised.

"That's how they mostly are," he observed. "If they aren't fightin' the law, they're fightin' amongst themselves. Colin was a fool to trust any of them."

Cliffy had no generalizations to make nor did he philosophize. He drove straight to the heart of the matter, saying: "All right. Then what we got to do now . . . is get Colin O'Brien. He's lyin' over there, afraid to charge us an' afraid to stay where he is." Cliffy reared back his head, looked up through the tree limbs at the blue sky, and said: "Fine. Now, then, let's get him."

Jim looked annoyed. "How?" he demanded.

"No big problem, sonny," said old Cliffy. "You two sneak around and open up on 'em out back of 'em where I was. Me . . . I'll be waiting right here."

"They'll kill you sure," snorted Jim.

Cliffy lowered his head. He was smiling. "I've done this before and no one's kilt me yet. See them limbs up there? Well, that's where I'll be waiting, plumb hid out of sight. They'll come rushing along, lookin' everywhere . . . but up. Now let's get moving."

Cliffy stepped over to a shaggy old bull pine, measured the height to the lowest limb, and spat upon his hands. Jim and Given exchanged a silent look. Given grinned again and nodded.

"I think, if it hadn't been for Cliffy, we'd have lost out more than once in this fight. Let's go, Jim."

The last view Given and Crawford had of old Cliffy was just before his bedraggled nightshirt disappeared up through the limbs of the shaggy old bull pine. They swung southward after that, crossed over into the eastward forest, and started on around behind O'Brien's position. There was hardly a sound in the forest until a horse nickered and Jim Crawford, in the lead, broke over into a quick little trot. Given kept up easily as they passed from tree to tree, from sage to chaparral clumps, and halted eventually, down about where they'd first seen Cliffy after the capture of Bill Freitas.

The two remaining tied horses were still standing there, but they were no longer drowsing; they were peering intently up through the nearest trees. Given touched Jim's arm, stepped on ahead, and began a slow, silent advance inward. He and Jim were still 100 feet southward of the horses.

Given halted abruptly, faded out in a brush clump, raised his six-gun, and waited. Jim did not see anything, not for a while, but eventually he did. Two men were creeping toward the horses. They had been seen by the animals sometime earlier, which had apparently caused one of the beasts to nicker.

Jim put his lips to Given's ear. "That one at the back . . . that's O'Brien. You want to spook 'em over toward Cliffy?"

Given shook his head without turning it. He kept his gun poised and ready to fire. For a moment those two skulkers paused out of sight as though aware of their imminent peril but also as though they recognized that now they had no alternative other than to make a final dash for those horses on ahead.

Crawford got flat down, raised his carbine, snugged it back, and lowered his head. He was ready to track the rustlers over his front sight.

The man with O'Brien suddenly halted and stood up. The tension had been too much; the almost certain death awaiting him had broken this outlaw's will. He threw down his gun and started to turn westward, facing in the direction of his enemies. O'Brien,

223

probably believing his companion was about to shout, to call out that he surrendered, sprang up with an oath and lunged. The other man moved swiftly to his left and swung. O'Brien ran head-on into that sledging fist. His hat flew one way, his fisted .45 flew another direction. He went ahead, carried along by momentum, crashed into a tree, and bounced backward, fell, and flopped over onto his back.

Given stood up. "Steady," he said quietly, his gun muzzle aimed low. "Steady, cowboy. Go check him for a hide-out, Jim."

Crawford went on across. The rustler didn't move, didn't speak or even change expression. He had a soggy, torn trouser leg where a bullet had evidently creased him. When Jim finished his search, stepped clear, and put up his six-gun, the rustler turned, spat, turned back, and looked dispassionately at the unconscious Colin O'Brien. He said huskily: "Ain't no amount of money on earth worth gettin' killed over, and that damned fool's been leadin' us in a losin' fight ever since we left the ranch. All right, Deputy, you got me. Now what?"

Jim looked at Given. The ex-lawman said: "We'd better contact Haines. We've got a long ride ahead of us."

Jim nodded, and wordlessly turned away. As he strode off, Given bent, picked up O'Brien's gun, ripped open the unconscious man's shirt, unbuckled O'Brien's money belt, and yanked it loose. O'Brien flopped and moaned but otherwise did not move.

224

"Fourteen thousand in there," muttered the demoralized Swallowtail rider. "You wouldn't be interested in splittin' it an' cuttin' out of here on these two horses before your friends get back?"

Given flung the thick belt over his shoulder, holstered his gun, and gazed at the lone survivor in an expressionless way. "Want a little advice?" he asked. "Don't get talked into something as stupid as this again."

"Stupid . . . ?"

"Yeah. O'Brien only thought he was smart, cowboy. Greed tripped him up. If he'd gone on with the fourteen thousand, he'd probably have made it clean out of the country. When he figured to take a long chance and maybe wind up rich by stealing the cattle, he was just plain stupid. It never could've worked."

"Don't worry," mumbled the range rider. "I've learned."

Given motioned downward. "Take off his belts and use them to tie his arms behind his back."

While the conscious rustler was tying the unconscious one, Bill and Jim came back with the horses. Bill was arguing about something.

"Up in a *tree?* What in the hell is he doing up in a tree?"

Jim looked at Given and slyly winked. He then reached up to scratch his head and mutter in that slow Arkansas drawl of his: "Now that you mention it, Bill, it *is* sort of late to be buildin' a nest, isn't it?"

Haines swore and glared downward. But he only shot O'Brien and the other prisoner one scathing glance, then said to Given: "Tell me what Cliffy's doin' up in a tree, will you, Ed?"

Cliffy himself came strolling up. "Huntin' your breakfast," he said, "you danged old ingrate." He walked past, gazed at Colin O'Brien, and blew out a long breath. "I didn't really want to shoot him, anyway. I'm glad it turned out like this. I heard you talkin' to 'em, Mister Given, and clumb down. Those dog-gone needles sure are stickery, too." Cliffy turned, eyed the tied horses, and shrugged. "Well, expect I might as well cut saddle strings and get to patchin' up *cinchas*." He started to move off, thought of something else, and turned back. "Mister Given, that fat money belt over your shoulder there . . . it wouldn't happen to have my three thousand dollars in it, would it?"

Given took down the belt and tossed it over to the older man. "Count it for yourself," he said. "I didn't look inside."

Bill Haines came boiling down out of his saddle. "Now, just a damned minute, you old nanny goat. We'll *both* count that money!"

O'Brien came around as his former companion in the cattle-stealing enterprise finished tying him and got back upright. O'Brien didn't at first see the men from Younger standing behind him. He called the other captive a hard name and started to say something else, then he caught sight of two sets of booted, spurred feet from the edge of his eye, slowly turned his head, and slowly lifted his eyes. Given and Deputy Crawford were stonily regarding him. O'Brien's breath ran out of him.

The other prisoner said, "Greedy damned fool," and stalked on over to halt near Jim Crawford. "They tell me, if a feller spills his guts about something illegal, Deputy, the law goes easier on him. Is that right?"

Jim looked at the man, thought a moment, then slowly nodded. "Yeah, it's right. But there's one drawback. We only have one state prison in Oregon, and, if you turn state's evidence, you're still going to wind up in the same hoosegow with O'Brien and Freitas and anyone else who's left alive. I'd sort of think it over if I were you."

The cowboy turned and scornfully stared at O'Brien. "Hell," he growled, "I'll take my chances with O'Brien. He only thinks he's tough."

Given made a correction. "He's tough, all right. He's just not very smart."

Bill Haines stood up with a fist full of money. He was smiling, but his swollen, bloody face with its soggy bandage made the smile look like a frightful leer. Bill was unaware of this, though, as he said: "It's all here. Ed Given, I never thought I'd see the day I'd be glad to be associated with you, but that just shows how damned wrong a man can be."

Given said quietly: "Don't thank me, Ed. It's Cliffy who saved that money for you. Cliffy and the deputy here."

Haines felt inside his shirt for the wallet with his other money in it. As he did this, he said: "Listen, you three, free drinks at the Territorial Saloon any time you want 'em for the rest of your lousy lives, an' I mean every word of it, too. Free drinks for life."

Cliffy, stuffing money into his nightshirt pocket, looked hard at Haines. "You're just sayin' that because you feel good right now, Bill Haines, but I know you . . . you'd skin your own grandmother at that crummy bar you run."

Haines turned. The big vein in his neck swelled; his scarred and battered features darkened. He opened his mouth, hung fire for a moment, then slowly smiled. "Of all the no-account old devils I ever saw who wear *pink*-striped nightshirts, Cliffy Hart, you're the prettiest I ever lay eyes on. I got a notion to kiss you."

"Here," squawked the liveryman, backing up hastily. "Here now, what's the matter with you? Get away from me or I'll tell everyone in town you . . ."

Given laughed aloud. The others turned and looked at him. Jim grinned and shrugged. None of them had heard Given laugh before, but it was a good, rich sound. "I reckon we'd better get astride, hadn't we?" Jim asked, still grinning. "What'll we do . . . hunt up the hurt and dead and haul 'em back or bury them here . . . those as needs it?"

"Haul 'em back," said Given, sobering. "Then there's a couple more things to be done. Eat breakfast at O'Brien's camp and, after that, round up the herd and drift it back toward the Swallowtail range."

"Oh, no," groaned Haines, all his earlier exuberance winking out. "I'm so sick of saddle leather I swear I'll never leave my saloon again. Ed, why can't we just head the herd in the right direction and, when we get back, get Cuff to send some of his boys down here to drift it on home?"

"Because," said Given solemnly, "I've always wanted to see someone with your past driving *honest* cattle, Bill. That'll make my visit here complete."

Cliffy's eyes sprang wide open. "Visit? Marshal, you aren't sayin' you're not goin' to stay in the Younger country, are you?"

"I'm staying, Cliffy. I've got a young pardner back in town, waiting for me. We're going out and look over some pieces of land. I meant my visit to *this* part of the Younger country."

Given walked over and took the reins to the Swallowtail horse he'd ridden and tested the *cincha*, stepped in, and swung up. "I'll go over and start the fire. You boys fetch in the prisoners. And, Cliffy, you've got the nose for it. See if there are any others besides Freitas still alive." Given turned and reined away.

Jim Crawford watched the ex-lawman weave in and out of the trees. He said: "Bill, I was thinkin' of resignin' as deputy sheriff at Younger. But with *him* around, I think I'll just stay on."

Cliffy, holding the money belt in one hand, his Winchester in the other hand, wagged his head. "That's the only decent thing that ever come out of Bill Haines's settlin' in these parts . . . attractin' a feller like Ed Given."

Haines spun around.

Cliffy wagged his finger. "Remember," he cooed, "I saved your lousy money for you. If you insult me, next time I won't get it back for you."

Before Bill could say anything he'd later regret, Jim stepped over and yanked Colin O'Brien to his feet, saying: "Give me a hand with these two, Bill. Cliffy, go do like the marshal said. Hunt up the rest of O'Brien's scruffy crew."

About the Author

Lauran Paine who, under his own name and various pseudonyms has written over nine hundred books, was born in Duluth, Minnesota, a descendant of the Revolutionary War patriot and author, Thomas Paine. His family moved to California when he was at a young age and his apprenticeship as a Western writer came about through the years he spent in the livestock trade, rodeos, and even motion pictures where he served as an extra because of his expert horsemanship in several films starring movie cowboy Johnny Mack Brown. In the late 1930s, Paine trapped wild horses in northern Arizona and even, for a time, worked as a professional farrier. Paine came to know the Old West through the eyes of many who had been born in the previous century, and he learned that Western life had been very different from the way it was portrayed on the screen. "I knew men who had killed other men," he later recalled. "But they were the exceptions. Prior to and during the Depression, people were just too busy eking out an existence to indulge in Saturday-night brawls." He served in the U.S. Navy in the Second World War and began writing for Western pulp magazines following his discharge. It is interesting to note that all of his earliest novels (written under his own name and the pseudonym Mark Carrel) were published in the British market and he soon had as strong a following in that country as in the United States. Paine's Western fiction is characterized by strong plots, authenticity, an apparently effortless ability to construct situation and character, and a preference for building his stories upon a solid foundation of historical fact. *Adobe Empire* (1956), one of his best novels, is a fictionalized account of the last twenty years in the life of trader William Bent and, in an off-trail way, has a melancholy, bittersweet texture that is not easily forgotten. In later novels like *The White Bird* (Five Star Westerns, 1997) and *Cache Cañon* (Five Star Westerns, 1998), he has shown that the special magic and power of his stories and characters have only matured along with his basic themes of changing times, changing attitudes, learning from experience, respecting nature, and the yearning for a simpler, more moderate way of life.